Black Horse Down & Other Stories

Black Horse Down & Other Stories

Ashok Ahlawat

THE BROWSER | FAUJI DAYS

Title: Black Horse Down & Other Stories
Author: Ashok Ahlawat

ISBN: 978-93-92210-75-4

Published by:
JGS Enterprises Pvt Ltd
Imprint: The Browser | Fauji Days

Publisher's Address:
SCO 14-15, FF, Sector 8-C, Chandigarh 160 009

Website: thebrowser.org
Email: service@thebrowser.in

Disclaimer:
All names, characters, and incidents portrayed in this work are fictitious. No identification with actual persons (living or deceased), places, buildings, and products is intended or should be inferred.

THE BROWSER
Publishers & Booksellers

FAUJI DAYS
Oral History and Military Publishing

Contents

Black Horse Down

A new priest had arrived in the unit, and the Commandant, a man who believed in keeping the gods happy, was not long in calling him to his house.

The pandit *ji* was reputed to have repaired the teetering careers of many senior officers. One supremo even took him everywhere with him on postings and would not take any step without checking the hiccups of constellations and the mood of the gods. The Commandant got *boondi* laddoos made in *desi* ghee and cardamom-flavoured tea made for the refreshment of the priest, then took a bath and wore his spotless white *kurta-pyjama* to await the arrival of the man who could talk to the stars and hear the whispers of the gods. He had sent his black Ambassador car for the priest and had also gotten a fresh can of Ganga *jal*, just in case his fortunes needed to be washed.

The priest had a short *bodi* but a large girth from where his day started. He ate six laddoos while his Wi-Fi receiver was warming up to catch the whisperings of the celestial bodies. The Commandant sat with serenity and waited for the learned man to start. The priest drank a cup of tea, opened his charts, and asked the officer, 'Sahib, have you lost anything costly recently?'

The Commandant scratched his head and considered whether the loss of a pair of slippers that his pet Labrador had hidden in the large garden of the Flagstaff house be considered a significant loss.

'Not really, pandit ji, but recently, the value of my shares invested in MDH chicken masala company has fallen badly.'

'Tch tch, Sahib, that is all because of Shani standing in the seventh house of Rahu. Do you also feel angry all the time and worried about your ACR?' asked the pandit ji.

'Pandit ji, you have absolutely diagnosed my condition. I keep feeling angry from morning till evening, and I am not sure about my coming ACR despite my best efforts.'

'Sahib, there is no time to be lost. Lord Shani is not very happy with you. I will tell you an *upaay*. You must go to the temple every day and pray and after that feed *gud* and *chana* to a black horse for 30 days – non-stop – and after that light a mustard oil lamp under a peepal tree.'

The pandit ji collected his *dakshina* of ₹501, said 'Hari Om', 'Hari Om' three times, and the black Ambassador dropped him home.

Every morning, the Commandant started going to the equitation stables, carrying a bag of gram and jaggery and fed the black horse affectionately. He and the black horse seemed friends from a past life.

One fine day, the sugar levels of the black horse shot up from eating kilos of jaggery, and he sat down and closed his eyes and never got up again. The Head Risaldar of the horses called up the young Captain who was the Equitation Officer and said, 'Sir, there is one small bad news: the black horse is very unwell.'

The Equitation Officer put on his khaki pith helmet, kicked his motorcycle, flew down the Trishul and past Gole Market, and shot into the ivy-covered horse-shoe arch of the equitation lines. Risaldar Hanuman Singh gave him a bow-legged, clicking salute and led him to the Troop Number One stable, where the black horse lay silent and unmoving. The Equitation Officer went and checked his pulse. There was no pulse beat in the shining black horse.

The hours dragged, and the Captain scratched his head. The next day, the Commandant would come with his bag of *gur* and *chana*. The incident was grave, and he thought he must report it to the Commandant. He called up the Colonel Admin and asked him to arrange his meeting with the Commandant.

The Commandant's office was huge. When the Captain entered and stood at attention, the Commandant, a tiny man, was sitting behind a huge desk, and only his head showed above the desk.

'Yes, why did you want to see me?' he asked tersely.

The Captain steeled his nerves and said, 'Sir, I have good news for you.'

'What's the good news?'

'Sir, that black horse has died.'

The Commandant sat stunned as if struck on the head by a policeman's baton. Then he screamed in anger, 'Is this a bloody joke? How dare you call it good news! It's very bad news and I will not leave you for this. How dare you let the black horse die. You will pay dearly for this.'

The Commandant was in a fury.

The Captain was wily and quick-witted, and like Birbal explaining a thing to Akbar, he said, 'Sir, it's good news because your Shani had been transferred to the black horse, and that's why he died, and now you are a free man.'

Suddenly the Commandant started laughing and jumping in joy and thumping his desk. He congratulated the Captain and said he would strongly recommend him for the Chief's commendation card and that he was the best instructor in the whole of NDA.

The Captain took a deep breath, saluted the Commandant, and came out. When he got back to the equitation lines, the Risaldar of the horses met him, 'Sahib, how was the meeting with the Commandant Sahib?'

'Sahib, for the present, things are taken care of, but I am sure his Shani will again return. Do we have another completely black horse?'

'Sahib, we have that horse called Pickpocket, but one of his legs is white; the rest of him is completely black,' said the Equitation JCO.

The young Captain said, 'Sahib, paint Pickpocket's leg black for I suspect Shani won't be long in reappearing.'

Match-fixing

A new officer had joined the regiment and since he was an English peer, or viscount, or something of that sort, he was given the Adjutant's chair by the Commandant.

One day, he was heard shouting the RM's[1] name from his office desk and he probably expected the RM to come running to him.

'Mansa Ram, Mansa Ram. Where the hell is this fellow Mansa Ram?' he called out and started puffing at his pipe.

It sounded like he was calling out for someone called 'Mansa Rum'. He was new to India, and although it was October, he was perspiring, and his khaki tunic was as wet as it would be on a *dhobi*'s slab.

Down the veranda, the RM of the 14th Bengal Lancers (Murray's Jat Lancers) was talking to the head clerk and heard his name being called by the new Adjutant. He continued

1. Risaldar Major's. The RM rank was equivalent to a Subedar Major's rank in the infantry.

speaking to the other VCO[2] and ignored the calls until after a few minutes when a *sowar*[3] came to inform that the Adjutant Sahib wanted to see him.

The RM got up and went to the Adjutant's office.

'Didn't you hear me? I was calling out for you,' said the new officer, not without irritation.

'No, I didn't.'

'But I clearly called out your name – Mansa Ram – several times,' said the new officer, lifting up the page on which he had noted down the names and appointments of all the Indian VCOs of the regiment.

'But Sahib, my name is not Mansa Ram,' replied the RM.

Now it was the new officer's turn to be riled.

'What nonsense are you talking? Your name is Mansa Ram,' he said animated with irritation.

'Sahib, there are many men by the name of Mansa Ram in the regiment. One is a cook, and one is a daffadar[4] and then there are some others. My name is Risaldar Major Mansa Ram, Sahib.'

The officer gave the VCO a hard, malevolent stare and then smiled. There was a saying that went—beware the horns of a bull, heels of a horse, and the smile of an Englishman.

The Adjutant spoke, 'The Viceroy is visiting our station shortly. We have planned a polo match in his honour. One side will be British officers, and the other team will be Indian VCOs and men who play polo. The whole station will be there to watch.'

That evening, in the mess, the blond English peer asked other officers, 'How is the Indian polo string?'

---

2. Viceroy's Commissioned Officer

3. A sepoy was referred to as sowar in the cavalry

4. A sergeant was referred to as daffadar in the cavalry

'They are alright, but they have poor horses; they don't stand a chance against the officers' team. Also, they have only one formidable player. If he is checked, then the match will be ours.'

Days passed and the fateful day arrived. The Viceroy and Vice René came to Risalpur. There were parades, receptions, dinners, hunts, and balls. Then came the day of the polo match. The Commandant called the captain of the Indians and whispered something to him. The Indian seemed to have been stung by a wasp, but he nodded, saluted, and left quietly.

The fanfare played as the viceregal carriage, accompanied by the clatter and jingle of chains, pulled up. The trotting outriders halted, and the station commander greeted the Viceroy.

The Viceroy went and threw the ball between the lined-up ponies and polo players. It was a beautiful day, and a mild cool breeze blew down from the hills of the frontier. By the end of the third *chukker* (round), the English team was several goals up and the Adjutant, who was an English peer and a Viscount, asserted the white man's supremacy and rough-housed most of the Indian players. He then came riding out of the blue and bumped the RM's horse so hard that the Indian's horse staggered and sank to the ground. The Indian captain fell, and his turban rolled off his head. Before the umpire could blow the whistle, the timekeeper blew the bugle and the third chukker came to an end. The old Risaldar picked up his turban and led his horse off the field by the reins, walking alongside it.

At the other end, an English Major who was playing, rode up to the English Viscount and said, 'Why did you do that? It was uncalled for and a bad foul on your part. There was no need for that. We are easily winning the match and now you go and commit an unpardonable foul on the seniormost Indian player. You clearly don't know his nature and you don't know your own regiment.'

The young Englishman just shrugged his shoulders. 'It's polo and such things happen, and my horse just went and collided with his horse before I could do anything.'

At the Indian end of the polo field, Risaldar Major Mansa Ram said to his syce[5] Ram Kishen, '*Angrez ki chokkri hamen polo khelna sikha rahi hai. Toofan ko lagao.* (The English girl is teaching us how to play polo. Saddle up Toofan.)'

When the bugle blew for the fourth chukker and the teams lined up in front of the Viceroy's pavilion, Mansa Ram was seen sitting on his huge polo pony, Toofan.

The Indian team rammed home many goals and the Adjutant didn't come near the RM after he got the first taste of his own medicine. The game turned and the Indians won the match. There was a hushed silence, and the Viceroy got up and quietly left.

Later, the Commandant confronted the Risaldar Major.

'RM Sahib, I had asked you to lose the match. Then what happened to you in the fourth chukker? You played very well but that was not part of the plan.'

'Sahib, we were losing the match as ordered by you. But the young Sahib came and fouled me badly and when I was on the ground without my turban, he laughed at me. I had agreed to lose the match, but not my honour. Now, you may do whatever you deem fit.'

---

5. A syce was someone who groomed the horses

Risaldar Major Mansa Ram Ahlawat, IOM of the 14 Murray's Jat Lancers lost two of his real brothers in the First World War in Iraq. He was a seeded polo player and played in his regiment's A string. The 14th Bengal Lancers had one of the best polo teams in India. Risaldar Major Mansa Ram, from my village, Gocchi, died in 1962. This story was related to me by my father. RM Mansa Ram used to keep two buffaloes while in service so that the supply of good fresh milk was always there and anyone who came to visit him could be offered milk to drink. It seems tea was not much preferred in those days. My father also said that the English officer who was the Adjutant was posted to some other regiment after this incident as it was deemed that he was unfit to serve with the 14th Murray's Lancers.

Postman's Part

He had given his best to the day, and soon, he would switch off the bedside lamp and sleep. He liked sleeping early and getting up early. It was his habit. He was looking after a large chunk of the terrorist-infested mountains in the north, and his battalions were widely dispersed. Mountains need boots.

The familiar sounds of the night cicadas cricking in the bushes outside and the static electric buzz of the night's silence sang in his ear – the noise of stillness and peace he thought. A jackal started howling in the night, long and mournful calls as if it hadn't eaten a *langar poorie* for seven days. He ran over the events of the day, they came tumbling out like apples of habit. The Handycam of his subconscious re-wound and the PowerPoint of memory started, and he reviewed the day's slides for the weak link of the day. It had been a long day and now that all the telephone calls and information updating had been done and the shark of zero error fed, there was nothing more that he could do. It was time to sleep. He was a good soldier with a clear conscience. It was hard to keep a clear conscience in these quadcopter times. He had done all he could. A pattering sound came from the false ceiling of the roof and his ears cocked. 'Rats,' he thought. They danced over the white squares of the false ceiling. For some time, he heard the rats playing on the roof of his room and then he fell asleep.

It was the low beeping of the phone that woke him up. The bedside lamp was still on and the light on the phone told him that it was from the big boss. He looked at the quartz wall clock – it was half past one in the night. He cursed the boss silently, 'Does the man ever sleep?' He had been raining orders on him since the three Islamic terrorists had been spotted in the forests in his area. What did he want now at half past one in the night?

'Yes, Sir,' he answered, trying to control his voice but something inside him was quite peeved.

'Are you sleeping?' asked the boss.

'Yes, Sir,' he answered, holding back something else that he had been about to say. 'It is good,' he thought, 'this habit of patience and self-control.'

'It's the first time in your area that contact with terrorists has taken place. We must not miss this opportunity to earn laurels,' said the boss.

'Yes, Sir,' he replied while thinking, 'Why is he calling me up at half past one to tell me of this desire for laurels? I am the in-charge in this area, and I know what I am doing. Anyhow!' He thought the boss must have something pressing to have called at such a late hour. A nightjar called and he heard a hen cluck loudly as well. His house had a hen coop in which hens and roosters strutted about. The giant rooster that he had was one hell of a big bird. It was almost three feet tall, and all the hens seemed to love that rooster. 'Strange,' he thought; he was thinking about his rooster and his hens and bird behaviour when the boss was talking about the only thing he ever talked about – terrorists and kills.

'Do you have a map of the area where the battalion is in the jungles? I will tell you where to shift the cordons and stops. Open Google Maps on your computer. Have you opened it? Look, whenever I call you, you must immediately open the map sheet and Google Maps. Now, do you have it open?'

'Yes, Sir, I have it open and I am all ears. I also have a pencil and paper in my hands.'

The boss started discussing or rather lecturing him about the terrain, saddles, nullahs, escarpments, OGWs,[1] hideouts, jungles, spies and surveillance, and operations. He was in the know of all the teams and locations that were employed in the search for the terrorists. The mountains were high and vast. There were thousands of folds, spurs, caves, forests, scattered villages, shepherd huts, and *dhoks*.[2] The troops had been out in the jungles for many days. The big boss, who knew everything better than everybody else, had been pressing him to do everything as per his assessments because he was the big boss, and he was the best. The boss was a great boss and a great man, and he knew great tactics and great strategy and learnt in the best courses and schools of instruction all over the world. He had to listen to the boss, and he listened quietly.

'Move this team two kilometres to the north in this square. There was a telephone intercept here, here, and here, and if the terrorists try to break out from their hides, they are likely to go here, here, and here. We must block all their routes of escape here, here, here, and here. It's not for nothing that I attended NDC[3] from Fort Lukewarm and even topped it. They used to call me the Indian Von Clausewitz, the master of strategy. Ya, you will find out soon, when you exactly shift the troops,

1. Over-ground Workers

2. Dhoks area cluster of hutments, usually built by nomads

3. National Defence College

as I have explained. I hope I am clear. Put at least a platoon strength in this square of the map and three teams in these three nullahs.' There was a longish pause, after which the boss spoke again. 'Don't be surprised if I call you again within an hour and tell you to change the disposition of the troops on the ground. We must remain flexible. Flexibility is the key during such operations. That's what I learnt at Fort Lukewarm.'

The rats in the ceiling had gone to some remote corner of his tin cottage and were chewing at one of his woollen socks.He could hear them softly at it. He hoped they kept playing there and did not come and start jumping on the false ceiling, right where his bed was. He had scribbled the points of the boss on a pad and made some markings on his talc-sheet-covered map. He looked at them and then turned off the lamp and went to sleep. When he woke up, he saw the dim rays of dawn crest the hill. His king rooster let out a loud trumpeting call to announce the new day. He went and squeezed out some toothpaste on his brush and was about to start brushing his teeth when the phone rang. He knew it must be the boss again. He had a vague recollection of a dream he had in the night. His boss had been sitting on a highchair on a puffy cloud in the sky and was shouting, 'Kill! Kill! Kill!' Somewhat like a woodpecker's call. A strange dream, wonder what Freud would make of such a dream, he thought. He took his map and writing pad and went to his study adjoining the bedroom and picked up the phone.

'What's new? Any new developments? Have you got them?' asked the boss.

'No, Sir. Actually, I have just woken up and I was about to brush my teeth,' he answered truthfully.

'Look here, I just sleep for one hour during operations and I have been getting intelligence inputs from my sources in the night. Just go to Google Maps and note it down. I will tell you where to shift the cordons and which particular areas to comb today.'

The boss dictated the new coordinates of the areas in which he wanted army dogs to go, in which he wanted the Special Forces boys in beards to sit on trees, and where he wanted them to be part of the undergrowth in ghillie sniper suits.[4] He wanted hourly updates throughout the day without fail.

Once the call was done, he brushed his teeth, ate his omelette for breakfast, sharpened his Apsara pencils, and walked to his office. The day was long and monotonous. The troops were doing their jobs, the operation was going on, and the commander and officers were doing all they could. After giving his boss a dozen updates and taking down an endless stream of instructions during the course of the day, he came back to his tin cottage. The rooster had been standing in the lawn and when he came walking down the pathway, the rooster puffed his feathers and craned his neck. The damned bird was magnificent. His short life meant something to him, and he knew he had it very good. He had a harem of 24 hens, and even if he ended up as a chicken lollipop someday, he was living like a Mughal emperor.

He was preparing for another night, aware of the jolts and earfuls of the constant stream of intelligence and directions to come from the big boss. He sat and unlaced his green jungle boots and threw his socks aside. The ceiling was silent. Where had the rats gone? Why were they silent? The phone started ringing again. He picked up the phone and listened for a few minutes and then kept the phone down. It wasn't from the boss but from the commanding officer of the battalion in the jungle.

He was towelling himself after a bath when the phone started ringing again. This time, it was the boss, and he started off as usual. 'Start noting down where I want the cordons to be put

---

4. A ghillie suit is a type of camouflage clothing designed to resemble the background environment – such as foliage, snow, or sand.

for the night and where I want the troops to sit in ambushes tonight. Not a moment is to be wasted. Time is of the utmost importance and flexibility is the key.'

He said, 'Sir I have some news for you. All three terrorists have been found and taken care of without any losses to our own side. I have told the CO to wind up.'

There was a triumphant chuckle from the other end of the phone, 'Well, well! This is what I was expecting. It all went off as per my design. It happens when you follow my directions well. I guided you all the way and I managed the whole show. Wasn't I magnificent and so much in control of the whole operation? And now we have three grand successes. What do you have to say to that? You must admit that it was all because of me. You just had a postman's part in the whole operation, conveying my directions down to the CO.'

He was quiet for some time. He wondered what to say to the Indian Von Clausewitz. He could again hear the rats gnawing something in the false ceiling of his tin hut. He wished he was standing in front of his boss, face to face, for he wanted to see his boss' expression when he heard what he was about to tell him.

'Sir I have to tell you something. I didn't implement or pass down even one single direction of yours down the chain. Not even one. I didn't breathe down any subordinate's neck and allowed them to get on with their jobs undisturbed.'

A Higher Courage

I came on leave from the field, and I found the 'buddy' (erstwhile 'batman' authorised to an Army officer) hadn't shaved. I saw him for a few days and asked, 'Why are you keeping a beard?'

'I am going to visit the Tirupati Temple when I go on leave.'

The buddy was a gentle, soft-spoken boy who couldn't harm an ant. He had made good friends with both my tiny Chihuahua dogs. Many a time, I saw him lift them both and carry them down the stairs from our first-floor house. The Chihuahuas had come to the house after a long and protracted siege when I had dug in my feet and told my wife and daughter, 'Either I live in the house or dogs.' Mother and daughter duo unanimously decreed dogs were preferable to me because I left the house messier than dogs could ever do. Since I was given the choice of *vanvaas*, the MS Branch[1] happily obliged me when I stated my problem to my Colonel MS.

---

1. Military Secretary Branch that handles postings and transfers

'Sir, don't worry, we are here to help all officers facing such issues of *dharamsankat* at home. We will give you a compassionate ground posting to a class one field station to your entire satisfaction.'

People unnecessarily give names like 'Mama Shakuni Branch' and 'Mysterious Selection Branch' to the most noble and fair MS Branch. Within no time, I got a signal that I had been posted to a far-off place of which I had never heard and which was sure to rattle all my 24 vertebrates in travel and ironclad the seat of my bottom for the remainder of my life, like a rhesus monkey.

Now, in the house in front of ours, lives a huge Alsatian who drags along the person who takes him out on a leash. These days, their *aayah*'s father-in-law, who lives in the servants' quarter, takes the Alsatian for his walks. He is a *mariyal* old man in ill health who smokes *beedi*s all day long and drinks the daily *pauwaah* of hooch. Gulab Singh is a harmless old fellow, but I doubt if he weighs much more than the Alsatian himself. Many times, I have seen him standing next to his Activa scooter, continuously pressing the self-starter and then giving up, to sit on the ground and smoke a peaceful beedi, the fumes of which reach me on the balcony.

Today, my buddy took our two Chihuahuas on the leash, and the two little dogs bolted down, barking their cutting and shrill bark at everybody. Chihuahuas think they are the masters of the world and have no idea of their own vulnerability. They are rude little creatures.

Immediately after the Chihuahuas went down, the neighbour's door opened, and the huge and ferocious Alsatian came out, dragging Gulab Singh. Holding on to the leash for all he was worth and then, to prevent himself from falling headfirst on the stairs, Gulab Singh let go of the Alsatian's leash.

The Alsatian flew down the stairs and, in four leaps, had one of the tiny Chihuahuas in its mouth. I was watching all this from the balcony. I thought this was the end of the Chihuahua as I knew how dangerous an angry Alsatian could be. Only the head of my tiny Chihuahua was partly visible in the Alsatian's mouth, its button eyes looking larger than ever.

The boy who wanted to go to Tirupati bent down and grabbed the snarling Alsatian's ear and lifted him by the ear with one hand. The Alsatian started yelping, and the Tirupati-boy took out the Chihuahua from the Alsatian's mouth. and gave a kick to the huge Alsatian, which took off yelping. Luckily, the Chihuahua wasn't much injured.

Later, I asked the mild-natured Tirupati-boy, 'Weren't you afraid of the Alsatian?'

'*Mujhe nahi pata, Sir, lekin* Chihuahua *itna chota hai, uske saath kuch bhi ho sakta tha* (I don't know, Sir, but the Chihuahua is so small, anything could have happened to him).'

I wondered all throughout the day whether I would have done what he did under the circumstances and if I could have matched his sense of duty. He, with his boy's face and shining eyes and broken Hindi and Tirupati-beard.

'*Mera ko to kuch nahi, itna chota kutta ko kuch ho jaata to.*' The more I thought, the more I realised that he had a higher courage, a courage higher than mine.

The Old Man and God

High up in the mountains of Pir Panchal there lived an old man with his old wife. His only son had left him and had gone to the Gulf sultanates to work and earn the gold Dinar. He had wanted his son to work in the Rashtriya Rifles company as a porter, but the boy had bigger dreams than carrying cement sacks and eating oily *pooris* in the *langar*. The poor fellow had died there in an accident. but the old man kept waiting for his return and kept praying to Allah for his life, safety, and good health like all fathers.

Many years passed. Life became harder and harder for the old man as his body became weaker and weaker. But he prayed every day for his son's safe return. He could no longer work as hard, and people stopped hiring him. He had to think of something to keep the wolf of hunger away from his door. One day, he told his wife, 'By the grace of God, who is great and all-merciful, I will go to Poonch and buy things to start a tea stall on the track leading to Loran. Many travellers are hungry and thirsty on their way up, and if I sell tea and rusks to them, we will earn something this way.'

The wife was doubtful that her husband would be successful for he didn't know how to count, add, or subtract. However, she did not oppose it but said, 'I like your idea very much and, Allah willing, you will be successful.' She was a good wife and a companion of many decades to the old man.

People in the area slowly came to know that there was an old man's tea shack high up in the mountains on the remote track to Satharban and began visiting it. But as the grim tide of years passed, the couple became feebler. Then the old man's wife became sick, and he managed to carry her on his back down to the road. He thanked Allah for his mercy, grateful that he didn't slip and tumble headlong over the cliff. A few months passed in illness. He would look after her, cook *chapatis*, feed her, and then go back to his tea shack. Besides Allah and *namaaz*, she was his only companion to talk to and every evening, after he would come back, he would cook food and tell her about his day, and they would talk about their son and when he would come back.

Down below, in the far-off valley, where the Poonch River flowed over stones and jingling pebbles, an Army Major was taking a haircut in his Rashtriya Rifles battalion. The barber was a thick-armed Maratha soldier who kneaded and drummed the head after clipping the hair. Major Vijay Singh sat under a radiant picture of Katrina Kaif looking at him from the wall. The barber's fingers were dipped in opium, and Vijay soon fell asleep while the barber's fingers kept playing the keys on his head, neck and shoulders. After the haircut was done, Vijay wore his jacket and went to the waiting truck that would drop him and his group of soldiers at the end of the road. From there, they would climb up, on foot, for two days, to reach their company operating base. The narrow road was broken, and passing vehicles raised whirlwinds of sand. In no time they were all covered with dust, feeling happy when they finally jumped down from the sand-blasted truck.

The party of soldiers was loaded up like sherpas going to the Everest base camp. Vijay was going to relieve another officer, and the jawans were to relieve other personnel of the company operating base. They spread out and started climbing up the hills. With their assault rifles on the ready and heavy sherpa loads on their backs, they climbed up in silence. As the air became rarer, the sound made by their protesting lungs became so loud that it could be heard in their eardrums from the inner side.

After hours of climbing, the party was sore-backed and very tired. They sat down. There was nobody around and the last house was just a speck down below, sunlight glinting off its roof. A three-striped Havildar came to Vijay and said, 'Sahib, I know that there is a tea shack some way up. It is run by an old man. I am sure we can get tea there. Let's go there; it's just five minutes uphill from here.'

So, they moved again, grunts and creaks coming from the armour-plated and ruck-sacked young men. The tea shop came into view, tucked underneath a boulder, made of stone and mud. Its door was shut, and there was no smoke coming out of the black hole in the wall that served as the chimney. A plastic can stood next to a tin funnel in the hillside through which a thin trickle of water fell on the pebbly floor. In the stillness of the scene, the steady trickle of the mountain stream issuing from the tin funnel was loud and peaceful. The jawans went and opened their mouths wide and bent and stood under the funnel and drank water and splashed it on their faces and beards. The Havildar stood in front of the door and looked at it. He was surprised to see that it was not locked. So, he opened the latch and went in, along with a few other men. The only beam of light that was coming into the room was through the two holes in the primitive interiors hewn from soot-blackened wood and stone. Motes shone in the beam of light in the dark shop. A poster calendar on the wall with some verses of the Quran fluttered in the wind that entered the room as Vijay stepped inside the shop.

The owner was not there but there was milk in a pan and tea leaves and sugar in a plastic jar. Also, there was kindling for fire laid next to the hearth stove. Soon, the jawans had made a good fire, and they brewed themselves sweet tea, feeling refreshed afterwards.

Vijay said, 'Okay, it is time to go.'

All the men strapped on their loads and went out. Vijay and his Havildar and a few other jawans stood in the shop. They had cleaned up and tidied the shop and washed the utensils. It was time to leave. Vijay's eyes fell on the little wooden cash box lying in the shop. He went and lifted the lid and saw that the box was empty. He looked around at the sparse interiors of the shop that had nothing in it. A gust of wind came and the poster with the verses scraped on the rough stone wall. Vijay took out his wallet and turned his back so that nobody could see what he was doing. Then they went out and latched the door shut. The Army patrol continued its long trudge up the endless mountain range.

After about two to three months, Vijay was on his way down with the same troops, and this time, when they neared the tea shop, they saw a plume of blue smoke coming out of the chimney holes. The party again stopped there to have tea. They saw an old man whose skin was deeply wrinkled and who walked with a stoop. He welcomed them with a smile and made them sit on the stone sill in his shop. Within a few minutes, he got them cups of good hot tea. Vijay, who was very cheerful by nature, started talking to the old man and the wind, which blows rather hard up in the mountains, again tossed the old calendar to and fro.

'Baba, what is written on this calendar?' he asked the old man.

'*Janab*, I cannot read but it is the word of God written on it,' answered the old man.

'What does it say?' asked the Major.

'Sahib, it says that the hand of God is above all. Do you believe in God, Major Sahib?' It was the old man's turn to ask the young man a question.

'Baba, I have studied advanced science, and I really am sorry to disappoint you, but I don't think I believe in God.'

Vijay's blunt answer hurt the old man deeply. The old man looked Vijay in the eyes for a long time, and Vijay could see and count the deep leathery wrinkles on his face. The old man spoke in a soft voice that reminded Vijay of his own grandfather. In fact, there was much in the old man's bearing and aged looks that reminded Vijay of his own grandfather.

A solitary tear fell from the old man's eyes, and he said, 'Major Sahib, you are young, and at your age, it is natural to question things and set beliefs. Life is very long, and one needs the blessings of God, for without the blessings of God, not even a blade of grass tremors. Two months ago, my wife was on her deathbed, and I thought she was seeing the Grim Reaper approach. If she was taken away, I knew I would soon follow her. I am a very poor man without any children now. I had a son who left me to work out of the country, and he never came back. Now, I run this tea shop for livelihood. That day, I had not two Rupees on me, and my wife was dying. I went begging door-to-door but nobody gave me even ten Rupees. Nobody gives money to old people. I was at the end of my tether, and I fell on my knees and prayed to Allah to help me – to save my wife's life – for nothing happens on this Earth without His will. That evening, when I came back, tired and disappointed, to my shop, I had lost all hope. "This was the end," I thought. But that day, when I sat in this very place and looked up at this old calendar, it fluttered in the wind as it does now. I felt there was something different in my shop. It was clean and broomed, and all the utensils were clean and lined up neatly on the stone shelf. My eyes fell on that little cash box over there. I went to it and opened it. It was the way I had left it. My fingers shivered uncontrollably as they hovered to lift its lid and when I opened the box, there was a thick wad of notes in the box. There were 10,000 Rupees in it, and I had left it empty without a *paie* in it! God had come to this poor man's shop, Major Sahib. Do you still believe there is no God? I was able to get my wife treated, and she is much better now, Major Sahib. Do you still think there is no God?'

Vijay passed a stern look to all the soldiers who stood about listening to the old man and his God. The look clearly implied, 'All of you will keep your mouth shut.'

The Army Major paid the old man and picked up his AK-47, the patrol spread out, and the scouts took the lead. The wind again blew the old poster on the stones that said, 'The hand of God is above all things.'

Polishing Her Shoes

There was pitting on the toe leather of her shoes. Tiny holes had formed on the toe strip and the soles had rubbed plain. I didn't expect her new Liberty shoes to wear out so fast. She is a girl with her own Gen Z views but I am an old father from times when unquestioned obedience was the norm.

'Not much life left in these shoes, darling.' I said as I sat on the floor of our tiny balcony, cleaning her shoes. The Chihuahuas played about her legs, wagging love and welcome.

I had gone down as she was parking her scooty to inquire how her exams had been. She had wrinkled her nose, stretched her lips sideways, and expressed displeasure. I had asked her again and she had replied with a more inscrutable contortion of her face that clearly told me that I was asking unwanted and silly questions.

'I had a marvellous day at school. *Pata hai*, papa, I received two love letters. I am very popular in school. They just leave love letters in the school bag, and I don't know who has written the letters.'

'But, my darling, you study in an all-girls' school!'

'So?'

I shut my mouth.

'I had so much fun today, but don't ask me about my exam. It was such a fun day at school.'

When she came to this school five years ago, she did not have a single friend and felt ostracised. The adjustment was cruel, as it is on *fauji* kids. Nobody wanted to accept her in their narrow frog circles. I suggested to her that she should aim to pass out as the school captain one day from this very school.

'I have not eaten my tiffin and now mamma is going to fry me. Papa, take out my tiffin and empty it, please. Mamma shouldn't come to know.'

A man's loyalty towards his wife and daughter is a flexible rubber band seat on the fence. But she eats too much junk, and I worry. She is an ace swimmer and rifle shooter, but the kid has a penchant for too much chocolate and crisps. She throws her bag on the box settee, and I take her shoes off, which have a good amount of sand sticking to them.

I sit dabbing her black Liberty shoes with Cherry Blossom.

'You know you need a dusting cloth, a brush for dirt removal, and a finer brush for applying and shining the polish. It's quite an enjoyable thing once you start doing it – to see your own hands turn a dirty pair of shoes into a shining pair of shoes.'

But her thoughts are elsewhere.

'*Pataa hai* papa, *I you know na, ek baat batau*, I like keeping my sports shoes spick and span, but I don't care about my black school shoes.'

'Hmm,' I thought. 'How do I tell her that it would be nice if she kept her school shoes also spick and span?' But this pair had worn out rather quickly. I thought that it must be because of their swimming coach making them run more, now that they were senior girls and in the main string of the school's swimming team. 'Liberty has started making poor quality shoes. We got these shoes just two months ago. In our days, not even physical NDA[1] *ragda* used to wear out Liberty shoes. My friend and coursemate, JD Singh's shoe size used to be 12 or 13. The NDA quartermaster didn't have his shoe size, so he was allowed to wear Force 10 shoes of Liberty brand throughout training. Those shoes were very solid. And look at these things that Liberty is selling these days. They don't have a life of even two months,' I said.

My daughter replied, 'But papa, this is not the same new pair you got; only the model is the same. You see, papa, we have to take off our shoes outside the art studio in our school. You know how much I love art; I go there almost every day. On the very first day that I wore my new shoes to school and went to the art studio, that very day when I came out, I saw that my new shoes were missing. I went to my class teacher and complained. She said, "It's impossible to find out who stole your shoes. All students wear the same model of Liberty shoes." I asked my teacher, "Ma'am, I am barefooted. What am I to do?" The teacher said, "You do one thing – go back to the art studio and just pick up any pair of shoes that fits you." So, I went and found this pair of shoes that you are polishing now and, as you can see, it is quite worn out. Papa, I am sure that if you get me another new pair, that will also get nicked in no time.'

I polished her shoes till they glittered and kept my mouth shut instead of giving her my pearls of wisdom. It's better to let kids handle their own problems.

1. National Defence Academy

Eight Is Normal

Three officers who had served together in the *paltan*[1] sat together, talking of old times, which are the best times to talk about.

The topic started when Bobby Sir was talking about meeting his prospective bride for the first time. Ma'am sat listening. He had a thick and broad leather belt tied around his back to keep his vertebrae supported. He had been living with a broken back for years now, but that is another story. The future Mrs Bobby sat smiling on a chair in front of us.

Bobby Sir said, 'When I went to see her at her home, she asked me, "Do you drink?" I replied in my Malyali-accented Hindi, "Yes, I am a fauji, and I drink every day (*Daroo to me peete hai aur har roz peete hai*)." "How much?" she had asked me. "I drink eight large of Old Monk every day, I don't believe in God-Shod and religion, and I will die by the age of 40."'

1. Regiment

The drink spilt out of my mouth. I had heard of many match-making pitches, but this was the next level.

Mrs Bobby, a fervid churchgoer, said, 'All the boys I had seen had said only nice things about themselves. He was the first person who said things honestly and openly about himself. I started praying for his soul, and I said yes to marrying him.'

We were sitting in General Singh's drawing room. He had been following a diet and exercise plan successfully for over a year now and looked very fit. He also had an injured back problem that he had been keeping in check with yoga. And no, they didn't have a fat-disability bonus coming every month in their pension because in the *paltan*, there was no culture of reporting sick.

I had been nursing my glass of whisky for over an hour when he said, 'Ashok if you don't like the drink, you can go and throw it in the sink.'

I made apologetic noises about the high honour that I felt for single malt whisky and took a couple of quick sips.

Then he said, 'Eight large used to be a normal for me. I remember in Palampur, I had just cleared my staff college exam and came in a competitive vacancy. The God-feeling was not long in coming. There was some brigade dinner where all officers and the Commander had been invited. The evening wore on, the food was laid, and I was standing with a drink in my hands when the Commander passed me and said, "Come, Singh, let's go and have dinner."

'I looked at my glass and waved him on, saying, "Sir, *aap chalo, hum aate hain* (you go and have dinner, I will come later)."

'The Commander must have thought that I was slightly high, and so he said nothing more and quietly went to the dining hall. The next day I was called by the Commander to his office. "What was it that you meant yesterday? You were drunk." I did not know if the last one was a question or a statement. But I replied to it, nevertheless. "No, Sir, I was not drunk. I had just started my drinks." "No, but you were high." "No, Sir, I had just started having a drink." "What's your normal quota, Singh?" "Sir, eight large is normal, sometimes I have ten large also."

'The Brigade Commander looked at me with owl-like eyes and mouth open. "*Hain* (What)? Eight large?" "Yes, Sir, even during my staff college preparations, I used to have at least two smalls every day. I am too rational by nature, and only a couple of drinks make me feel like a human being." "Okay, you may go." When I came back, I realised he would seal my career for sure. He was the Brigade Commander. "ACR *me ragad dega*," I had thought.

'A few days later, there was an inter-battalion basketball game, and you know how Gorkhas play basketball. So, it was Aziz and me, the two officers, alone, and we won the basketball tournament. The next day, the Commander, who had seen the match, called me to his office. I went in, fearing that he still carried the grudge from the dinner. But he got up from his chair, shook my hands, and congratulated me for playing excellent basketball. He had a beautifully wrapped gift for me. "This is for you. You brought your team out of the brink of defeat." I opened the wrapping, and it turned out to be a beautiful bottle of Peter Scot whisky. I thanked him. He said very pleasantly, "But, remember, my dear Singh, you shouldn't tell your Brigade Commander to go and have dinner and that you will join him afterwards after having eight large."'

The Power of Old Monk

I call him up during my evening walk to pass the time. My friend is a gossipmonger with few parallels and often shares unusual stories with me. He is posted in the remote northeastern region of our country, and I am in the remote north, separated by just 2000 miles of India.

Our friendship goes back to the early 1990s, when we were both cadets in NDA, and used to go for a quick run to crown the events of the day after dinner at nine from the Ashoka Pillar Circle to the Pashan Gate and back. He was a swifter runner than me and still is. It was his wonky idea to gallop to Pashan Gate and back after dinner, on a full stomach, to become super good runners aiming for cross-country medallions. He did get his cross-country medal, but I remained a third enclosure runner during all my six terms in NDA.

'How is the new general?' I asked him.

He had gone for the dining in party of his new general the day before.

'*Badaa hie simple aadmi hai* (He is a simple man),' he replied.

'What makes you say so?'

I was surprised because my phlegmatic friend was never so charitable about praising someone, and if he said a good word about someone, then that person would have passed through a series of weighing-ins and litmus tests in his mind.

He continued, 'We asked him, "Sir, which whisky would you like to have – Glenlivet, Rampur, Black Label, Jack Daniel, or Glenfiddich?" "I don't drink much nowadays, and whisky never," was his calm and polite reply.

'"Come on, Sir, it's your first day in your new command." We still kept insisting that he have a drink. He mulled over the choices, and after a grave and a long pause, he said, "Okay, if you are so kind, I won't mind a small of Old Monk, please."'

We had been speaking on the phone as I walked around the polo grounds of 61 Cavalry. I was on leave from up north, and my wife and daughter were 'separate-familiying'[1] in the beautiful pink city. The polo ponies stampeded across the turf, and their hooves thudded on the carpet of grass. Then came the distinct click of a polo stick connecting with the white ball, the rapid drumbeat of 16 hoofs punched the earth, and horsemen galloped after the little white ball.

'What are you saying? He asked for Old Monk of all things?' I said, quite astonished by the humble tot of rum that the general desired.

'Yes, he did, and when he had his glass in his hands, he got talking to some of us who were standing with him and started telling an old story of the time when he had just joined his battalion in Jodhpur or Jaisalmer. "I don't remember which station," he said, "It was either of the two, and this is how the

---

1. When officers are posted in field areas, their families are allotted separated-family accommodation in a city

story goes. Many years ago, sometime in the late 1980s, six young officers sat drinking in their battalion mess on a very hot evening. The evening was so hot that the mess interiors were like a brick kiln, and the walls were baking in a high fever. In those days, the hot and the cold weather were faced without air conditioners and electric heating. The fan rotated unhelpfully on the ceiling and sent off gusts of hot air.

'"One of the young officers started cursing the heat after having a drink and shouted that he was fed up with the blasted heat that never relented and made their life a hell. He wished they were somewhere else, just anywhere away from that bloody burning hell. Overhead, the crooked and cunning old MES[2] fan, which last had its bearings greased when Jodhpur State Forces had merged with the Indian Army in 1952, clattered on its awry wings – *fatrr, fatrr, fatrr* – and sent down gust after gust of hot irritation that set off the officer's cursing. 'Like, where do you want to go, dear *Shehzaade* (prince),' teased his senior subaltern who had survived the past hot season in the station. 'Sir, anywhere except this blasted place where the heat never goes down,' said the young man, staring long at the political map of India that hung on the wall of the mess, next to the ubiquitous painting of Bonaparte on a rearing horse in the battle of Austerlitz, that he would later realise, ends up miraculously decorating every mess of the Indian army. 'Take it easy, lads, we are Indians; the heat and dust of our land are quite okay; drink up your glasses of old monk and recharge, and we will go out on the lawn. There is a desert breeze blowing outside at this time. Let's go out, it's cooler outside.'

'"The senior sub told the perspiring mess havildar to take the *bandobust* to the lawn bar. In a few minutes, the green field telephone set that works by cranking and the sundry chairs,

2. Military Engineering Service

peg tables, bottles, flasks, ice boxes, jugs, cigarette boxes, etc., were carried out to the lawn bar by the mess staff next to the defunct fountain, that lay dry because of shortage of water, and a burnt out tullu pump. One officer sat on the lawn chair and complained that even those chairs were so hot. The young men had had a good game of football with the jawans in the evening games parade. And they all had a big appetite. The mess havildar came and announced, 'Sahib, all eggs are finished and eaten.' 'You do you have potatoes and onions, right? Get some *pakoras* made,' said the senior subaltern to the mess havildar.

'"The young men kept drinking, gossiping, yarning, and nibbling pakoras. Then one fellow, whom wanderlust overcame after a few drinks, got up and said loudly, 'Sir, *kahin jaane ka mann kar raha hai* (I want to go somewhere).' The senior subaltern said, 'Okay, do one thing. Get the map of India from the mess.' The fresh Second Lieutenant went in and, under the bemused gaze of Napoleon, unhooked the political map of India from the wall, carried it outside and laid it on the low table. 'Tell me, where do you want to go?' 'Sir, I will tell you in a while.' By then, it was around half past nine. The senior subaltern got up and telephoned the battalion's second-in-command (2IC) and requested permission to go out. The 2IC, who had guessed that the youngsters were making it merry in the mess, replied, 'Don't drink and disturb your seniors,' and slammed the phone down without giving them any lift. The senior sub came back, and the six youngsters kept drinking and partying.

'"By 11 p.m. the officer again remembered that he had wanted to go somewhere. His desire and wanderlust again resurfaced. 'Sir, I want to go somewhere.' 'You are sure you do?' 'Absolutely, Sir.' The senior subaltern got up and tied a hanky around the Second Lieutenant's eyes. Then he said to him, 'Place your index finger on any spot on the map of India. Wherever your finger comes to rest, we will go there.' The other officers cheered loudly at what the senior sub had proposed, and the blindfolded Second Lieutenant placed his finger on the map. Everybody peered at the spot on the map and cheered loudly. 'Boy-o-boy, sure we will go here.' The senior subaltern again got up and went to the phone to telephone the 2IC. 'Sir, request permission to go out.' The 2IC said, 'Do whatever you want to do but let me sleep, dammit. Don't call and disturb me again.'

'"The senior subaltern went and said to the waiting officers, 'Okay, guys, we have got the permission. Let's go.' At about midnight, the Mess Havildar, who lay on a cot in the open, heard six motorcycle engines start, and then he heard the departing echoes of the Bullets, Yezdis, and Jaawa motorcycles. He turned in his bed, perspiring, and went off to sleep. He was used to young officers starting their motorcycles at midnight.

'"The next day, in the morning-PT fall-in, six officers were missing. The CO asked the 2IC, 'Any idea where these six buggers are?' The 2IC stood scratching his head and was extremely puzzled, 'Sir, they did call me up in the night and said they wanted to go out.' 'What did you say?' 'Sir, I was sleepy, and it's their daily joke to disturb seniors. I just told them to do whatever they wanted but let me sleep and not disturb me again.'

'"The CO did not report the matter up the chain. After about a week, the Corps Commander called him up and said, 'Well done, old chap, the GOC just called me up from Leh. Six of your youngsters sought accommodation from his ADC, and they are on motorcycles and are being well looked after. I will have a felicitation ceremony for them once they reach back here in Central Hall. Strange, though, that nobody informed me about this motorcycle expedition planned by your battalion. Very good show, I must say. First rate show, old chap. Well done.'

'"When the six youngsters of the Grenadiers battalion came back, the Corps Commander called all officers of the station and Corps HQ in a function and said to them, 'Here, look at these outstanding young officers. They are living their life, whereas all of you guys are just dead, you keep pushing paper and files from morning till evening. They went all the way up to Leh on their bikes, and that is the kind of spirit I appreciate in my young officers.'

'"It's a different matter that the CO had a different sort of reception in mind for the self-willed half dozen. For the next two weeks, all six of them went on a 40 km route march, in full battle loads, every day!"'

By now I was standing on one side of the walking track, wiping my sweat and half-wondering if I should blindfold myself and place myself in front of India's map or not as well. But first, I had to hear the story's finale.

'Once the General had finished his story, he said, "Do you know who the Second Lieutenant was who had put his finger on Leh on the map of India that night? It was me under the power of the Old Monk."'

Field Marshal Ka Successor

The movie *Sam Bahadur* takes us on a kaleidoscopic journey through the life and times of the effervescent Field Marshal and his disarmingly good humour and candour. It reaffirms our faith in moustaches *sans* beard, all the old and good values of a family, and the fact that people should marry out of love and compatibility and, as I do believe, till death do them part.

I got a new tune to whistle after watching the movie. The other day my daughter caught me whistling, *Sabka banda hai ye, rab ka banda hai ye* while I was brewing morning tea. I can't sing very well, but whistling gives me light-hearted joy, and I lapse into whistling often without conscious effort.

No, I have not changed my profession, and I am not planning to become a movie critic. I am here to write another little vignette out of the blank pages of history on which events were written with invisible ink. And the topic is again about Sam Maneckshaw and his times. I was not even born then, but an older gentleman friend, who was a witness to these events, wants me to engrave them in his words:

Throughout his life, the Field Marshal remained eternally grateful to the nursing officers. He could be anywhere in the country, but he would always try to make it to Wellington to attend the MNS[1] Corps Day. This was his way of showing eternal gratitude to the nurses who had looked after him when he was recovering from his previous wounds during the Second World War in Burma. On one such Corps Day, I was told to look after the bar and offer drinks to the Field Marshal. He used to have only two small drinks, and that was it. That evening, when he was alone, I said to him, 'Sir, may I ask you a question?'

'Shoot.' he said.

'Sir, why did the Government delay in making you a Field Marshal? It was as if it was an afterthought on the part of the Government.'

He stood thinking for ten long seconds, pondering on the question in his mind that this young Captain of the Army Medical Corps had asked him. Then, with a twinkle in his eyes, he raised his left index finger, placed it on his mouth, and said, 'To keep this mouth shut.'

I couldn't make much of this answer. I assumed that the Field Marshal was trying to tell me that I should keep my mouth shut. Later, after more contemplation, I realised that what the Field Marshal meant was that a Field Marshal never retired, and so it was assumed that Sam would never openly question the Government's decisions or offer resistance to the dictates of the *dhotiwallahs*.

'The Army lost out on a first-class Army Chief' was how Sam reacted when he learnt that Lieutenant General Prem

1. Military Nursing Service

Bhagat was not to succeed him as Army Chief. The non-descript political appointee Bewoor happily slid into the meshed chair of the Chief of Army Staff. In a video reel of the event, he can be seen throwing his arms towards the sky. Probably this gesture was meant to say, '*Meri galati hai kya, agar mujhe Chief bana diya? Sab bhagwan ki kripa hai* (Is it my fault that I am being made Chief? It's God's gift).' (For God read Indira Gandhi.)

There was an incident that had rattled Indira Gandhi. She was always fearful of the Indian Army throwing her into jail and taking over the country, as was being consistently done in Pakistan. After all, its officers were products of the same pre-partition British Indian Army and had the same thought processes and values. She often wondered how their Pakistani friends and counterparts could kick aside prime ministers so casually, like kicking a football on a playing field, and what really stopped them from copying their Pakistani counterparts. The need of the hour was to clip the wings of the Army since it enjoyed tremendous prestige in the aftermath of the 1971 victory. Indira was a dictatress wearing a saree. She was adept at removing thorns silently but ultimately paid the price of her follies by being bitten by the snake that she had raised to divide Hindu and Sikh votes and unity in Punjab.

The Army knew Lieutenant General Prem Bhagat, a Victoria Cross winner from the Second World War, as the next Chief following Maneckshaw. Northern Command was set up in June 1972, and Bhagat was appointed the Northern Army Commander. Somewhere around this time, Prime Minister Indira Gandhi came back from Srinagar by road and halted at the Command Headquarters in Uddhampur for the night. There was a social function in the station in the evening in which the families and kids of the station were in attendance along with many serving personnel. Both Indira Gandhi and Prem Bhagat were present in this function and sitting on a raised stage. The Army Commander took the mike and addressed the gathering: 'Our magnanimous Prime Minister, as a reward for the victory of 1971, will, now, provide funds for the accommodation for soldiers and their families in forward field areas in Jammu and Kashmir, so that, even while serving in remote frontiers, they can live with their families.' Indira Gandhi was livid with anger when she heard Prem Bhagat's announcement. She took the mike and said very coldly, 'Your Army Commander is putting words into my mouth. I have made no such commitment so far, and I will see what we can do.'

Then she got up and left the function. She had formed the impression that this man would prove equally intractable as Sam Maneckshaw where preserving the manor of the Army was concerned. Later, what she did was to send Prem Bhagat to Damodar Valley Corporation to supervise the construction of a dam, instead of making him the Army Chief after Sam. Another thorn had been removed.

Two months after Sam's retirement and anointment as the Field Marshal, the Third Pay Commission's recommendations were made public. Bewoor, the Army Chief, instead of offering his resignation as Sam would have offered to Indira Gandhi, accepted the Army's demotion in pay, perks, status, pension, etc., without a whimper.

Field Marshal Ki Beti

I was the Duty Medical Officer at the Military Hospital at Wellington that day. The sick report OPD was going on, and I was rubbing the stethoscope over an old man's back when a medical orderly came and said, 'Sir, there is a phone call for you.'

'Whose phone call is it?'

'Sir, I don't know. He said he was some Field Major and wanted to speak to the Duty Medical Officer. I couldn't catch his name.'

I pushed my chair back, got up, and walked to the MI room's[1] phone.

'Duty Medical Officer Captain Wahi speaking,' I said.

'Captain, this is Field Marshal Maneckshaw. My daughter is quite unwell, and I am soon getting her to the hospital. She is running high fever. I hope you will make her alright.'

I said, 'Sir, we will do our best.'

1. Medical Inspection Room

I had just come on posting to the Military Hospital Wellington, where the Defence Services Staff College is located, and I had heard that the nation's greatest hero, Field Marshal Sam Manekshaw, stayed somewhere nearby, but I had never expected to hear the unforgettable voice myself one of these days. I informed the Commandant of the hospital, and the medical specialist was asked to be on standby. Then came a flurry of activity of getting a good room aired, linen changed, and freshened up for the Field Marshal's daughter in the officer's family ward. We only had half an hour's notice. I raced to the ward to see the room and to brief the ward sister on duty about the important patient who we were about to receive.

As soon as I came back to my OPD room, I saw a grey Sunbeam Rapier car come and park at the hospital's common parking. The Field Marshal and his Gorkha batman were assisting a young lady out of the car. We put her on a wheeled stretcher trolley, got her to the OPD room, and helped her lie down on the bed. I noticed that the Field Marshal was nattily dressed in a jacket and a tie and his thinning silver hair was brilliantined and groomed backwards from his forehead. His daughter had a much simpler dressing sense. Also, whereas the Field Marshal was slim and elegant, his daughter was shorter in height. To put the patient at ease, we doctors often carry out small talk with our patients. I felt the pulse of the young lady and noticed that she had strong thick wrists and short fingers. The Field Marshal stood behind, watching me for some time, and then he went out. I felt relieved, because who can be absolutely at ease in the presence of the great Sam Maneckshaw? The young lady was burning with high fever. She was well behaved and silent all the while and I admired the way the Field Marshal had groomed his daughter in such an admirable and stoic manner.

I started feeling the heat of professional responsibility. I had to be absolutely spot-on about my diagnosis. There was no margin for error. I wanted to do the best for my patient especially when the patient was a pretty young lady who happened to be the daughter of the one and only Sam Maneckshaw. The Field Marshal's batman, surprisingly, was acting very possessive about the young lady. He wouldn't leave her side, and that was a hindrance to me. I told him curtly, '*Aye, tum udhar door jaa ke khada ho* (Hey, you go afar and stand there).'

The man sullenly withdrew to a corner but kept staring at the Field Marshal's daughter. I found this most odd and made a mental note about quietly slipping in my opinion about the batman to the Field Marshall. Frankly, I found it rather ridiculous that a batman should have the gall to stare at an officer's daughter like this. He needed to send that lecherous chap straight back to his battalion.

I turned back to my fair patient and asked her, 'Good morning, Ma'am. I am Captain Wahi. May I know your name, please?'

The young lady gave me a blank look. It happens many times in a doctor's life that a patient is disoriented by illness and fever.

I smiled softly at her and again asked her very politely, 'Good morning, Ma'am. How are you feeling? What is your name?'

The Field Marshal's daughter again refused to reply and turned her head slightly and looked at the batman. There was something in the young lady's look that raised a niggling doubt in my mind.

'Could the Field Marshal's daughter be having an affair with his batman?' God forbid me for thinking of such a thought, but at that time, a strong doubt of possibility crossed my mind. My resolve to report the batman as an evil snake stealing the affection of the Field Marshal's daughter became stronger and stronger.

I again asked her politely, 'Good morning, Ma'am. I am Captain Wahi. May I know your name, please?'

Suddenly the young lady shouted, '*Thaa chai Naa, tha chai Naa.*'

I couldn't catch her name properly. It sounded like 'Taa' and 'China'. Again the young lady and the batman were looking at each other and the Field Marshal's batman came forward towards me and said, 'Sir, my wife does not understand English. If you don't mind, I will interpret it for you. Her name is Dhan Maya.'

'Oh my God!' I thought. 'I have been such an utter idiot. Of course! The young lady was Mongoloid looking. How could she be the Field Marshal's daughter.' I started laughing loudly, and then I thought, 'Oh hell! A bed needs to be readied in the PBOR[2] family ward, and it had better be good because the Field Marshal is sure to come to see his daughter when she is recovering from her illness.'

Such was India's Field Marshal Sam Maneckshaw.

2. Personnel Below Officer Rank

The Field Marshal's Driver

There is this story about Field Marshal Sam Maneckshaw's driver when Maneckshaw was the Army Chief. The Army Chief must have had more than one dedicated driver for his official duties. Military drivers are also authorised leave of absence. This man was from Haryana, and his name was Shyam Singh.

One day, General Maneckshaw had come out laughing from a conference in the North Block. The driver, who was standing at rigid attention, opened the door for him. It was the month of April, and it was a fine mellow day with a balmy sun.

'*Tumhe pata hai*, Shyam Singh (You know Shyam Singh), the Defence Minister changed my name today. He called me Shyam. He said "Shyam, *maan bhi jao*."'

Babu Jagjivan Ram, the Defence Minister, had pleaded with Sam Maneckshaw to invade East Pakistan in April 1971 on Mrs Gandhi's insistence, and Sam had prophesied a 100 per cent defeat if the Indian Army went inside at that time.

'*Waise* there is not much difference in "Shyam" and "Sam". Just the letters "H" and "Y",' the future Field Marshal had chuckled.

After the war was over, just when General Maneckshaw was about to retire, he noticed Shyam Singh had become tense and his uneasiness was smeared on his face, which the General easily read.

'What's the matter, Shyam Singh? Your face, these days, looks like your family's buffalo has stopped giving milk?'

'Nahi, Sahib, *woh baat nahi hai* (No, Sir, that's not the matter).' The dour man would clamp shut.

The days passed, and Sam Maneckshaw's date of retirement came closer and closer. One day, the driver said, 'Sahib, I have one favour to ask of you, and only you can help me.'

'Yes, shoot, Shyam Singh.'

'Sahib, I want to go on retirement. Please help me obtain release from Army service.'

'But what's the matter? Do you have some *zameen kaa muqqadma* (land-based lawsuit) or some other family problems? You should try to serve your full length of service,' advised the Chief.

'*Nahi*, Sahib. That's not the matter. It's something else that I cannot disclose before I get my release from service.'

Maneckshaw appreciated the man's candour and did what he had to do, and the driver's release date and papers came. He asked his driver again, '*Ab to khush ho*? Tell me now why you have left service early.'

The driver stood at attention and said, 'Sahib, *aap ki gaadi chalane ke baad me kissi aur ki gaadi nahi chala sakta* (Sir, after being your driver, I cannot drive anyone else in my lifetime).'

The Field Marshal laughed and said, '*Tum bahut bada bewakoof ho* (You are a big fool).'

But now that his driver's papers had come through, nothing could be done. The driver was an obstinate Haryanvi. A breed of men who never retracted once they made up their minds.

However, the issue kept lingering in the Chief's mind. So, one day, he asked his driver, 'What will you do after retirement?'

'Sir, I will do something or the other. I will find a job,' replied the driver.

'How much agricultural land do you have?'

'None, Sir. I am from a poor family.'

The future Field Marshal was quite taken aback. This penniless poor man had just kicked his job because he couldn't drive another man after he had been a driver to him.

The day his driver was leaving, Sam gave him an envelope. 'Shyam Singh, open it only once you reach your home.'

'Ji, Sahib.' The driver saluted and left.

When he reached his home, he forgot all about the envelope and got busy with life and finding a job. He got a job of driving a freight truck.

One day, his wife said to him, 'I was putting away your Army uniform in the *sandook*, and this envelope was in your shirt pocket.'

'Oh, this! I had forgotten all about it. I did not open it because I can't read or write much. Sahib must have written a DO[1] letter of appreciation for me as is the practice with senior officers.'

'*Phir bhi*, please open it and have it read by the school masterji and tell me what it says.' said the wife.

So, the soldier and his wife went to the village school and requested the headmaster to translate the contents of the letter. The headmaster put on his glasses and tore open the envelope and his eyes stayed transfixed on the sheet of paper.

---

1. Demi Official

'Why are you staring at the page like this, masterji?' asked Shyam Singh.

'You have any idea what this letter is?'

'No, Sir, I don't.'

'This is a transfer deed. The Haryana Government had given a war *jagir* of 25 acres of land to General Sam Maneckshaw in Haryana after the 1971 war victory. He has gifted his war jagir to you. You are the owner of 25 acres of agricultural land now.'

The wife whacked her husband angrily. 'You fool! I was about to burn this envelope to light the *choolha*. Thank God, I asked you what was in it first.'

Chacha Lewis

English-less in an English School

To say what you want to say
You must create another language
And nourish it for years
With what you have loved
With what you have lost
With what you will never find again.

—George Seferis, a Greek poet

An English teacher who owned only two shirts and two pants and taught Indian students for almost 30 years without accepting any salary passed away in a solitary little house somewhere in France. His companions were bare walls, unloved poverty, faceless anonymity, and solitary, visitor-less life. He lived all alone with a cat.

When an old student of his managed to track him down in his hermit's hut in France in 2016, she was his first visitor in 12 years. Koval had been her student in the Delhi school where he had taught after Rai. He had once taken her to the World Book Fair at Pragati Maidan and had bought her books.

She stood outside his chimneyed one-roomed cottage in the precinct of Jumelles-Gouttes in south-central France. Grey plumes of smoke rose like words of welcome and homecoming from the chimney. There he stood tall and old with his shelves full of PG Wodehouse and the venerable Homer and Ovid and Sophocles and Horace.

'I want to make a documentary film on you.' she said.

'Why?'

'Because you are the most important man in my life,' she replied.

'Nobody is going to watch your film, and you are going to die broke like me.'

He had left his country and come to India – the land of heat, dust, superstition, colour, emotions, thousands of gods, snake charmers, rope trick, maharajas, beggars, forests with elephants and tigers, and deserts with camels. India pulsating with life and chaos – exactly as God intended life to be on Earth. He loved the old cycles of life and dreaded the race of machines that had so obsessed and enslaved the West. Why he came to teach in India remains an unsolved mystery.

I once asked one of his old students: 'Why do you think Mr Lewis came to teach in India of all places?'

He had scratched his chin and said, 'It was said of him that he didn't even get a postman's job in England, so he came to India.'

That's the kind of thing that over-imaginative Indian boys may give as a reason for an Englishman who had come to India to teach. The more bizarre the reason, the better!

Mr Yashpal Bhardwaj (YPB), the great visionary educator met Alan Lewis sometime in 1977 when he went to attend a teachers' conference in the UK. He saw Lewis' involvement in plays and declamation and his high devotion to teaching. YPB was a 'poacher' of the finest talent pool of teachers for Rai. Wherever he found a brilliant teacher, he dangled the hook and often managed to land the fish on the deck board of Rai. In Allan Lewis' case, YPB had landed a swordfish, as far as teachers went. Lewis was of a rare breed. He only worked for a small honorarium and not a full teacher's salary and with travel and daily allowances, and other allowances, which are allowed to a regular teacher on the Government list. But, my God, could that man work! He was a slogger. He never asked the students to carry notebooks to his house on the campus. He carried notebooks to correct, and the pile would be as high as two feet. He would go through each notebook with a 'fine-tooth comb', sifting errors, writing clarifications, and taking equal interest in every pupil's work, whether he was a bright spark or the class dud. In fact, he would take more interest in the duds.

He had the Englishman's dread of publicity. He came to teach English-less boys English at Rai School in 1977. He taught the language by instructing boys to read books and testing them through random questions about passages in them. Through plays and discussions at his house, and although I was far too young to grasp *Othello* and Shakespeare at that time, I had started learning 'A for apple, B for bat, and C for cat'. Then, we, first standard scholars, were marched to the auditorium to watch Mr Lewis' plays.

When the wooden horse came on the stage I would be sitting in the front row and wondering what new hell was about to descend on my tender sensibilities, what new scary scenes awaited us. The dark auditorium was a place of fear and dread. But I clearly remember the joy I felt when I saw the Trojan Horse pulled on the stage. It was a huge horse made of wooden planks. The curtain fell in the previous act. When the curtains slid apart again, there stood the Trojan Horse, solitary and pensive, staring at the city gate of Troy. When the night fell, and the Trojans were drunk from partying, out started jumping cutlased Greeks in short skirts and red plumed helmets out of the belly of the wooden horse. Almost 43 years later, as I write now, the thrill and the joy of the play seen as a first grader seeps my memory with the sweet wonder of that childhood evening.

The other week, they had shown us a movie with an octopus, and I had sweated in fear while trying to sleep. The underwater scenes of undersea divers grappling with giant squids and octopuses were a scary show but not the Trojan Horse and the stage where the mikes hung low from ceiling wires, like fruits on a creeper and students dressed in strange clothes came and spoke in some unintelligible language underneath the mikes. At that stage of my life, I couldn't even make out that they were speaking in English.

We used to be shepherded and asked to sit in the front-most row since we were the youngest boys and girls in the school. Today, we laugh over the times, but I don't think that those days were all ringing with joy. A five-year-old cannot even tie his shoelaces if he has only lived barefooted till then. A five-year-old cannot tie the drawstrings of his underwear if has only roamed around naked at home till then, and such a child cannot comprehend Troy's *Wooden Horse* or Shakespeare's *Macbeth*, the earliest plays of my life that I sat through in wonderment, my arms and fingers pulled over my eyes and sweat and fear oozing out of every pore of my body. It would have been much kinder if someone had just told me the synopsis of Troy's *Wooden Horse* or *Macbeth* and other plays and just assured me that there was nothing to fear. The actor-students were just making a racket and playing a role; they were not going to pounce on the little kids of class one sitting in the foremost row of seats right in front of the stage. Seats that swallowed the small boys and girls completely.

The older boys called him Chacha Lewis and feared his birch cane and, more often than not, ended up reading the books he gave them to read. Then they were called for *viva voce* from the book, and if Chacha discovered that they hadn't read and digested the book and were bluffing, he would offer you puttee parade or caning. Many boys opted for the cane whacks. They padded their bottoms with newspapers and additional underwear and took their punishments. He never whacked the girls. They were told to stand with their faces to the wall as punishment for not reading.

In 1989, Mr Yashpal Bhardwaj left the school, and Chacha Lewis followed soon after. One day, he landed up at Mr Baweja's school – Bal Bharti School, Pitampura. Mr Baweja was also an old Rai teacher who had shifted to Delhi.

'Hello, Mr Baweja. May I sit down?' said Allan Lewis. He had suddenly dropped from the sky.

Mr Baweja said, 'Yes, yes, please do. What a pleasant surprise.'

'I have left Rai am I looking for a job.' said Allan.

'Who told you that you are looking for a job? You are already working with me,' said Mr Baweja.

Lewis had a hearty laugh. He straightaway got into the school's teaching and took over the English Department as well as the task of setting up the new library of the school.

He never expected a salary or anything. That was so typical of the man. He was dismissive of the most important commodity in life – money. Bal Bharti started giving him a stipend of ₹5,000 a month, despite his resistance to the idea. He would spend all his money on his departmental colleagues and his students, getting them eats and books.

Mr Baweja recalls, 'All the 15 years that he worked at Bal Bharti, I saw him in his two pants and two shirts. I had asked him, "Allan, your clothes are made of what material? You are getting older, but your clothes never age." He smiled and said, "I am okay with only a few things only in life." Once, I had asked him, "Allan, why did you leave England and come to India?" He just said, "I hate England."'

Grammar, for him, was like the Gita and the Quran.

When he was about 75 years old and had to quit teaching, he withdrew to the Correze region in France, which lies between Bordeaux and Lyon. Koval last met him on 20 November 2023 in his house:

'He was very, very sick and weak at that time, and he was utterly lonely.

'He had often asked me, "Was I a very cruel teacher? Did I beat my students too much?" He had regrets.

'The biggest problem in his life seemed to be that he believed that nobody loved him. So, he was astonished when I first turned up at his door in 2016. He had believed all along that his students couldn't like him at all. I spent a lot of years trying to show how much he was loved. Who could love a cold recluse who was socially so awkward and who could never make friends with anyone?'

But in the end, it proved true of his life what the great psychoanalyst Carl Jung had said of honest work ethics, 'An old alchemist gave the following consolation to one of his disciples – no matter how isolated you are and how lonely you feel, if you do your work truly and conscientiously, unknown friends will come and seek you.'

Acknowledgements

My deepest thanks to the following people associated with Mr Allan Lewis' life and times, who warmly shared information with me that enabled me to write this essay.

1. *Mr Baweja, Bal Bharti School, Pitampura.*
2. *Mrs Mondira Bhardwaj.*
3. *Colonel Anil Amar, Alumni Rai.*
4. *Colonel Dinesh Chauhan, Alumni Rai.*
5. *Satish Sharma, Alumni Rai.*
6. *Ms Koval Bhatia, Alumni Bal Bharti School, Pitampura.*

I Think I Am Having a Heart Attack

This story was shared with me by a very fine General who recently retired as an Army Commander. I have had a long acquaintance with the general officer, and I found the story he was relating a fantastic, interesting story of courage and resilience.

The cold passed reluctantly from the earth, and the retiring fog revealed a young officer sitting on a roadside rock. A sky blue GREF[1] dumper truck rattled past, with ruddy-cheeked girls standing in the open carriage of the Tata truck. Their cheeks were blue and hard from the cold, and they stood in the truck, closely packed, going for their day's work. They all wore the same crude heavy green coat parka with woollen lining and a ringed hood. Everybody wore that crude coat there in those days, right from the porter boy who climbed to your

1. General Reserve Engineer Force

post carrying two Jerry cans of kerosene oil on his back with a strap around his head to you, the officer in charge on that post in the rocks from where you saw the white shark fin-like peak of the Chomo Lahri mountain sticking up from the grey carpet of clouds. On a clear day, you saw the Kanchenjunga with your left eye and the Chomo Lahri with the right eye, and the long Chinese stone barrack with tin roofs at the pass down below, puffs of pine log smoke floating out of their chimneys, if you dipped your head down. You felt like a solitary unwashed god who sat for hours over a kerosene primus stove, warming his fingers and eating dead tinned food.

These Sikkim girls were tough and strong and kept within their world of work and family. They were beautiful in their determination to laugh while breaking stones with hammers or when heating the tar coal drums with smoking rhodendron stumps. When they wore other clothes, one couldn't imagine that they broke stone to make gravel for the roads eight hours a day. Then they comported themselves like young girls fond of looking beautiful and wearing beautiful clothes. And then they looked very good indeed with their compact and fit physiques and ever wary of army soldiers who flirted with them and promised them marriage and bliss and Milkmaid tins and a never-ending supply of Old Monk rum.

I was waiting to bum a ride down in some Shaktiman (old Army three-ton truck) or a Nissan one-ton going to Gangtok. The snow had fallen, and the road had sheets of ice and snow. In those days, second lieutenants were bummers. They were left to their own devices to learn the ropes and manage, and it was a good thing, I say. I waved to a few trucks, but none seemed willing to take me and the few Gorkha soldiers who had also chosen the same cold day to go down from the high mountain. I thought that I would have to try my luck the next day as most of the vehicles had passed, and the timing for down vehicles was about to close. Then a lone Jonga came swaying on the ice with its wheels going *chiglik chiglik* with ice chains on the wheels singing. 'Some high officer going; not a frickin hope of a lift,' I thought.

The Jonga stopped, and the Brigade Major (BM), a tall rugged, handsome man of a make, mould, panache and sophistication that is no longer seen in the army, asked me, 'Where to dude?'

I was surprised because you are surprised as a one-pipper if someone even acknowledges your existence. I had seen the BM play volleyball with our Gorkha troops on my way up and down from the posts or some other dogsbody job.

'Sir, waiting for a lift to go down on leave to Gangtok, but no luck so far.'

'How many are you?'

'Sir, me and my three men.'

'Hop on, tell them to squeeze in.'

There were already men in the Jonga, but somehow my chaps sat on the tail board, and they squeezed in like vegetables in a grocery bag. The BM got behind the wheel, and I sat in front. We reached Siliguri by evening. For those of us who joined the army in the old days of train travel, getting a ride on the Assam Courier meant saving yourself two or three days of tedious train travel in stinking trains. So, thanks to that impromptu Jonga ride, I was saved a couple of days of tiresome travel in trains.

Later, I met the BM again. He had, by then, become an army commander and retired, but he kept himself busy with physical fitness activities and other social awareness pursuits, like cycling all along the Ganges, with a message to keep the river clean. Some stories have long breaks, but one tends to hold on to those unasked-for decencies done long ago, like one's first wristwatch, long after the expiry of the treasure phase of one's life.

Recently he returned from the mountains. His old mother needed his care. He had to take her to the Command Hospital for care and treatment. He would get up early in the morning and go for his long cycling, and then after looking after his mother, he would hurry off to the gym for his workouts.

For a couple of days, he had been feeling the birth of a new pain in his chest. The new pain was like a new sun exploding and whirling hot inside his ribs. Life had never been free of aches, injuries, and pains in a long service in the army. He had played all sports and had suffered his good share of knocks and tears and injuries in a long and active career in the army. He had climbed mountains, skydived from helicopters, and cycled for hundreds of kilometres all along the Ganges but never felt anything like this. He silently hoped that it would go away on its own, and for a few days, he ignored it and did his round of work.

The round circle of woes started when one day when his wife called him in panic and said, 'Someone has drugged mother, but I don't know by whom or how or when. She cannot recall anything, my name, your name. She doesn't recognise me. She is talking of things that I don't know, that I have no idea of.'

He took his mother to the military hospital the next day. They did her brain scans and found a large tumour in her brain that was rubbing her memory centre. His own chest, like Pompeii, felt under a restless Vesuvius. He had got some scans done from a civil hospital, and that day, he had gone to the army radiologist in the military hospital. He was wearing his gym gear and carrying his gym bag, and he planned to go straight to the gym from the hospital and bring his mother for radiation therapy at one o'clock.

The radiologist was talking to a line of jawans as part of his additional duties, who were lined up outside his office, and he had time to sit and think as he waited for the radiologist to get free. He thought, 'Here I have had this burning sensation in my chest for the last three days. I feel it's not a muscular pain or a structural pain. There is something wrong inside me, and here I am, sitting in a hospital. Why shouldn't I just show myself and get over this anxiety? What the hell is happening inside my chest?'

The general got up and walked to the hospital commandant's office further down the corridor. There was another general sitting with the commandant. They said hellos and the other visitor told him that it happened to be the hospital commandant's marriage anniversary.

In the general's own words, the conversation went like this:

~

'Good morning, Commandant! Wish you a very happy and blissful marriage anniversary, and I think I am having a heart attack. That's why I have come to you.'

The other two men looked at each other and smiled. They thought I was pulling their leg and joking.

The hospital commandant said, 'Sir, what are you saying? Heart attacks don't happen just like that. You are walking about merrily and declaring "I am having a heart attack" in gym clothes and smiling and chatting. Never saw anyone walking and talking and throwing in "O I think I am having a heart attack" in my 36 years of medical experience. But, anyhow, I will have you checked up for your satisfaction.'

So, they took me down to the Cath Lab and there were these young colonels, army medicos. I said to them, 'Good morning, guys! I think I am having a heart attack.'

These young doctors started laughing at me and said, 'Sir, you are joking, aren't you? Nobody has ever walked in gym clothes, carding a gym bag on his shoulders, and announced that he is having a heart attack.'

I was pretty annoyed that nobody was taking me seriously. So, I said, 'Well, guys, there is always a first time to everything. Why don't you have a look at me?'

With great reluctance and disbelief, they laid me out on a bed and stuck the ECG probes all over me. The machine burped out the jagged lines on the screen, and the cardiologist said, 'Oh, my god! Sir, you are right. You are having a heart attack right at this moment as you are talking to us.'

I said, 'I have been saying the same thing since the morning, haven't I? Nobody believed me.'

They gave me local anaesthesia and started operating on me to shove in the stents, and I felt like reciting Epicurus to them, so I said:

'Why should we fear death?
If I am death is not.
If death is I am not.
So why fear when both cannot coexist.'

After the operation, I thought, 'Alok Kler, you are lucky. You were there at the right place at the right time, due to your mother's illness. Strange and benevolent is the alliance of the gods with mothers. Even in their extreme illness, mothers somehow end up helping their kids. Thanks to your mother, you are alive today. If your heart would have capsized on some remote mountain somewhere, what would have happened then?'

Keys of Heaven

The imam was screaming '*haiya all fallah, haiya all fallah*', and Chaggan felt the hammering boom of the masjid's loudspeaker. He had been walking about searching for Julie, who had just disappeared. He was carrying a piece of chicken and bones in his pockets. The full moon had grown above the Ranjaati ridge and looked, from there, like a watchman, seeing what he was doing. He thought that only the moon knew that he was looking for Julie. As an afterthought, he wondered if the moon also knew that later in the night, he would go out. He had not told that to anyone. Not even his CO. He started whistling, but the dog was nowhere to be seen, and neither was there any sign of her three pups.

The imam of the village mosque was bombarding loud phrases anew. The imam never got tired of his screaming recitations, and he had the mouth of the loudspeakers trained at his post. Chaggan had learnt the verses by heart and enjoyed repeating them when the mullah blared his existence like a cockerel. The mullah screamed louder on full moon nights, like Bianaca Pointifiore from Herge's *Tin Tin* comics, he had a bad voice but never tired. Chaggan had hung the same twenty-rupee Arabic calendar with phases of the moon that he had seen in madrasas and masjids. The moon was saying hello from its chair on the mountaintop. A good night he thought, good enough for what he had in mind, and nobody knew about it.

He had inherited his secretiveness from his father, a major of the Army Intelligence Corps long dead. The memory of his parents came suddenly, unannounced, scenes of childhood that seemed resting right at his elbow. He had only to turn his neck and relive his past, his father reading to him about Kim Philby, the British head of MI 6 who had defected to the Soviet Union.

Your left hand shouldn't know what your right hand is upto in secret missions.

He had been fond of spies and detectives right from childhood, reading again and again all the Sherlock Holmes and Hercule Poirot stories. He laughed when he remembered what his father often said, looking at the slight bulge of his tummy: 'This is the only civilian part of my body, rest is under control.'

He clicked his fingers and started rubbing his hands. The winter was at its sharpest, and the *mannu* and *safeda* trees were all standing like skeletons without even a single leaf. The old porter of the post *salaamed* him and hurried on his way to his hut, his plastic shoes scraping on the gravel. Noori was a faithful old chap; he had been the porter of the post since he was a young man, and now, he was fifty. He was a *pucca mussalman*, and it was men like Noori who kept their heads devoid of getting diseased and unhinged on religious lines.

Noori needed work all the time. On the days there was nothing to do on the post, Noori would go around ranting in circles, 'Give me work to do, give me something to do, or I cannot eat my roti. I have to earn it to eat it.'

'Noori, you are a lunatic. Sit down in peace. You have worked enough all your life.'

'No, Sir, please give me work or send me to some other post.'

Then he had to create some work. 'Okay, dig a flowerbed in front of my hut and plant some flower seeds in it.'

He saw the old man's departing form duck out of the company gate. In Islam or Hinduism, a good man was a good man, he thought. To live in peace, he needed no more gods than the sun, moon, wind, and blue sky. He heard the sentry close the steel gate and then the sliding noise of the steel chain to secure it. But a herd needed a man welding a stick; the herd demanded it as a necessity.

It had been three months since he had come to Chaghcharan and taken charge of his company. The broken track ended here. The khaki hand of law ended 30 km away at Chist-e-Sharif. The mullahs here ranted on loudspeakers with their voice screaming about, '*khuda ka khauf* and day of judgement – what will you answer God on day of judgement?' They never let a day off without dragging God on all four legs and on a leash and into people's lives. This particular imam's screaming sermons could scare the Mumbai underworld and make them shift office space!

He went to his hut and ducked inside. He contemplated whether he should have a drink or not. The man he was waiting for might come or might not come. If he had one drink, he might feel like having another and then another. He looked at a hand fan made of date leaves that his mother had given him on his posting to Kashmir. '*Le, beta, pankha ley ja saath, hawa karr lena agar bijli nahi ho to* (Son, take this hand fan just in case electricity fails; it will come in handy).'

He had quietly kept the fan in his gear, and now it hung over his headrest on a nail. She had had a very difficult life as a lonely widow who had never gone to school.

There was a knock on his door.

'Ram, Ram, Sahib.' A voice called from the darkness.

'*As-salaam alaikum*, Sher Mohammad, *andar aa jao* (Hello, Sher Mohammad, come inside).'

'*Wa-alaikum salam*, Sir.'

A small, wiry man entered his hut. He wore a chocolate brown Pathan suit and had a long beard. Sher Mohammad looked like a shepherd boy or a hill farmer, whichever way one looked at him. He carried a backpack in which he had a pair of night-vision binoculars, a Kalashnikov, and a light blanket.

'It's been many days you have been away, *dost* (friend). Hope you have been keeping N's house under surveillance. Is N there in her house in Farasang? Sorry! I even forgot to offer you a drink. Will you have a drink, Sher Mohammad? I only have Old Monk here.'

'*Nahi*, Sahib. *Shukriya*. N's college is closing this week. She will be coming to Farasang soon. I am camping with my father's sheep there. It is good grazing in Farasang, and our sheep are becoming fatter and fatter.'

'Do you want to take a bath, Sher Mohammad? There's a tin of hot water in my *gusalkhana* (bathroom); you can have a bath, brother.'

'Nahi, Sahib, I am fine. I should smell like a Bakkarwal also! I know I must be smelling strongly of rancid butter, sweat, and sheep.'

'Sher Mohammad you are stinking like ten Bakkarwals, not one.'

'Then it's great, Sir. Nobody suspects a man who smells like ten Bakkarwals.'

'When will I see you again?'

'If your hunch is right, Sir, I will send my cousin Latif Laali to you. Then you must come, like the wind, with him.'

Nobody wanted to come to Chagcharan. The spread of his company was vast. He had come gladly and wanted to stay there as long as he could. He had a bag full of books – he wanted to read, and the intoxication of new learning drove him everyday. He woke up hungering for life with his eyes and his ears and his hands and legs. He wanted to see each and every rill and stream, rock and tree, and pool in his area. He climbed up to foaming waterfalls in the Pir Panchal. There were meadows smooth enough for Tiger Woods to come and practise putting. He carried his father's college prize book that had the poetry of 15 poets in it. He read Keat's *Endymion* in the hill glades, and he heard the naiads whispering, looking at him from the grove of mountain oaks overhanging the pool. He had been searching all the beauty spots of his domain that no man's foot had ever walked over.

The village of Farasang stood on the far ridge, and he was walking down a goat track. A giant Himalayan barbet was singing up in the *mannu* tree. Its belly was all brown and it was singing with the energy of Usain Bolt running the 100 m sprint. He looked at the bird with his Army binoculars for long, mesmerised by its plume. Then he moved on, and his batman, Balram, followed 20 paces behind him. He started down the trail, observing a blue whistling thrush. The thrush went and sat on a rock. Then his eyes saw two figures walking up the track. The thrush flew off and he went and stood behind the rock so that the people walking up couldn't see him. The girl was walking in front, and she was of medium height. She was thin, so she looked taller. She wore a dove-grey suit and an ivory cardigan. Suddenly, he stepped onto the path when the girl was a few strides away. The girl looked at him, and their eyes met; she kept walking. When the girl had crossed him, on an impulse he said, 'Please stop, miss.'

The girl stopped.

He walked up to her and stopped in front of her. 'I am Captain Chaggan from Chaghcharan. At your service.' He unslung his backpack and took out a big chocolate bar.

'I am Nilofer, daughter of Haji Nusrat of Farasang. That's my house up there.' The girl was pointing to a house up on the hill.

Chaggan gave her the chocolate and bowed to her. The girl smiled and started walking up.

'Inshallah, we shall meet again,' he said to the departing figure.

She looked over her shoulders once.

This had been months ago, and he had met Nilofer at her college.

'The *kaffir* again presents himself,' he had said to her, giving her a bouquet of red roses. He had carried them for her from Delhi and had waited for her outside the college gate in Jammu. The roses were a day old but looked fresh and beautiful.

'You are not one of the "faithfuls", mister,' she had chided him. 'My people will cut you into pieces if they come to know that you have come and met me,' she had teased him.

'So be it,' he said. 'Who cares as long I see you with my own eyes.'

He had gone up to Chaghcharan and positioned Sher Muhammad in Farsang with orders to keep Haji Nusrat's house under observation.

Three days later, Latif Laali came to him in the morning.

'Sahib, Sher Mohammad Bhai has sent me. We have to move immediately. Today the guests may come to Haji's house, and Nilofer is also there in Farsang.'

Chaggan took ten of his best men. They changed into Pathan suits, split into three small groups, reached Haji's house, and deployed in a half circle around the house. There was an outhouse of two rooms in which four men were talking.

'Haji has two daughters, and we are their guests. I have told him to send his daughters with the dinner to entertain us.'

The four men started laughing like hyaenas smelling meat.

Chaggan kicked the door in and fired a long burst. It was over in five seconds. Subedar Subhash came running with two *sepoys*.

'Sahib, are you alright? We heard a burst.'

Sher Mohammad came out of the room and said, 'Sahib, two are dead and two are injured but alive. I have tied them up.'

'Take off all their clothes and search every seam and fold of their clothing. I will be back in ten minutes.'

Chaggan went and knocked at Haji's door. The Haji opened the door and looked at him.

'You must be Captain Chaggan.'

'Yes, but we have never met before.'

'My daughter tells me everything. Please come in. Have you taken care of the "*mehmaans*"?'

'Yes, they are comfortable. They won't bother anyone again.'

Nilofer came out with her mother, and said, 'Mother, he is my friend, Chaggan. You know, Chaggan, I have secured admission in Jamia at Delhi.'

When Chaggan came back to the outhouse, the two terrorists had been stripped. From their necks hung a large steel key, each on a steel chain.

'Why are you wearing this key?' he asked the terrorist.

'I was issued this key after completing my Mujahideen training in Pakistan. The Major Sahib there has obtained signed receipts from us for these keys. These are very important keys.'

Then the terrorist shut up.

'Look, boy, you better tell the whole story and tell it fast.' Chaggan said sliding the safety catch of his Kalashnikov to the downmost position.

'Major Sahib told us that these keys are for our rooms in heaven, reserved for us. We won't have to wait in a queue. We can go and directly open our rooms with the key and there would be 72 *hoors* in our room waiting for us.'

'Then there is no point in making you wait too long then, is there?'

Two single shots rang out in the dead of the night, and the echo travelled far into the valley.

Lahore Waaley

'*Mainu hoon kuch yaad nahi* (I don't remember a thing).' He said that after a very long silence on the mobile phone. He had told the story only once before to his father and mother and a few others in 1971. His family's garrulous Punjabis broadcast it among relatives far and wide.

It did not fail to occur to Suri that if the story got round to the Army authorities, he might be in a rabbit hole. So, he locked his tongue forever and threw away the key into the Satluj River.

When he was asked about that incident on the fiftieth anniversary of the 1971 India-Pakistan war, the old curmudgeon decided to heed old poet Chaucer's advice: 'It is not good to let sleeping hounds wake'. But he remembered each moment of that day 50 years ago with clarity.

It was 22 June 1971. Suri was a Captain in an Engineer Regiment deployed along the Punjab border with Pakistan. Their regiment had been given the task of sealing vital areas from Pakistan by laying defensive minefields all along the International Border.

In Punjab, the grain harvest had been done, and vast open tracts stretched and yawned into one another's land. At places, the ground broke into sandy gullies that abounded in *sarkanda* grass, a tangled wilderness of *keekar,* and thorn scrub. The hot 'Indian' sun had burnt everything over the ground to a glistening sandy grey. Even the green tree canopies looked like the chlorophyll sap had been boiled and steamed out of the leaves. The *babool* trees bore round yellow flowers that merged in the harsh molten silver of the suns aspect.

Suri enjoyed these survey jobs whence he took the talc sheet-covered map case and Chinagraph pencils. He had marked the day's area and noted down the eight-figure grid references in his notebook. Then he loaded the short-angle iron pickets and wire rolls. Captain Suri was a careful planner of things. His haversack bulged with the round cylindrical shape of two bottles of Golden Eagle beer.

The team of three people set off in a jeep. That day's reconnaissance route was long, and he assumed it would be a tiring day's work. Soon the metalled road withered away into a rutted village track furrowed deep with large iron wheels of bullock carts of the farmers. The oil sump of the jeep scraped the dry clay.

'Get it out of the furrow, else something will break underneath the jeep,' he admonished the driver. The CO was glaringly strict when it came to the unit's vehicles sustaining any kind of damage. The road springs of the battle jeeps were hard. They squinched as the jeep tyres went in and out of the ruts.

The driver overtook a crawling bullock cart with the giant Ferris wheels revolving slowly. An ancient Sikh farmer with a silvery flowing beard and a loosely draped turban waved his ox-whip at them in greeting. He sat perched on the whippletree, and his thin, wiry legs dangled and swayed like pendulums. The cart receded, and Suri looked back. The giant cart pulled by sturdy white oxen had turned towards a squat village of mud brick houses. That was the last village – he checked his map and confirmed it. The jeep ran on, raising a tail of dust in its wake.

'Head for that tree over there,' he motioned to the driver. The ploughed fields had receded, and shallow gullies criss-crossed the ground. They reached the area he had highlighted with a blue circle. The jeep halted, and he got down. The frontier, he assumed, was still a mile farther. He started with the surveyor and, taking the compass bearing from the tree, he indicated the surveyor to sink in an iron picket that the man was carrying with a hammer. He took out a tape measure and started unrolling the long tape. They worked on a hot, sun-beaten day. He looked forward to the beer after finishing his work. The driver had followed them with a bundle on his shoulders.

A dry *nullah* ran through the dip in the ground. It was not marked on the map. He puzzled over this new development of geography. Was he on the right piece of land, he wondered? He motioned the two men to sit while he went over his map once again.

As he studied the metre map, he heard the clink and scratch of hob-nailed boots. He continued reading grid references from his notebook. Everything seemed alright.

Suddenly, his men jumped up.

'*Saabji, bhaago*, run for it.' shouted his driver. What was the man shouting? Why should he run? He flipped the canvas map cover and got up.

It was then that he saw the Pakistani soldiers pointing their rifles at him. His men stood frozen like marble statues. He didn't understand what was occurring. Where had these enemy soldiers come from? He was well within the Indian territory.

A JCO stepped forward and said, '*Janab abb aap hamarey mehmaan hain, challen.* (You are our guests come.)'

'But we are in Indian territory,' he protested with a slash of anger in his voice.

'*Thande raho*, Captain Sahib (Stay calm, Captain Sahib).' retorted the JCO in a steely tone.

'*Haath baandh do inke* (Tie them up).' he commanded his men. The Pakistani soldiers tied their hands tightly behind their backs.

'Move now.' he ordered.

'But you can't do this. You are intruding inside India.'

'No, Janab, you are well inside Pakistani territory. No point resisting. You will be shot. Why die for nothing? Just obey my orders and be good prisoners. No point in damn fool cinema heroics.'

He realised that there was no option but to do as he was told. A man walked in front and the three prisoners followed. They walked quietly for a mile and then entered a company's defensive trenches and sand-bagged position. The enemy soldiers threw big-eyed looks of astonishment at the green-clad men. 'Hindustani *kaidi*' he heard them shout to each other with relish. They reached a tent, which was under a clump of date palms.

'Stand here and don't move,' cautioned the Pakistani Army JCO-in-charge. The side flaps of the tent were rolled up and the sandy floor was sprinkled with water. The air was peppered with petrichor. An officer sat behind a field table signing papers. He saw the JCO salute and speak to the officer. The JCO came out and motioned him to enter. He walked in and stood in front of the officer. The Pakistani Major was reading a form, then he signed it, screwed his fountain pen, and put it in his breast pocket. He looked up and said, 'What brings you here, Captain? You will be our guests now.'

Suri was fazed by the casual way of address. The enemy Major seemed almost bored and disinterested.

'Your men violated the International Border and apprehended me by ingressing into Indian territory. I demand that I be sent back immediately.' Suri tried to show a bold face.

'What's the hurry, Captain Sahib? Stay as our guest for a while, now that you have come all the way.' The Major smiled and looked at him with fixed eyes for long. Suri saw a twitch in the eyes of the Major as he stared at Suri. 'Right then, what is your name, once again, and unit and army number?' demanded the Pakistani.

Suri gave his army number and name.

'I see, the old stale insistence upon the Geneva Convention, is it? What unit do you belong to?' insisted the Pakistani.

'Yes, we go by the Geneva Convention. I am supposed to tell you only this much.'

'We will see about that. Krishan Mohan Suri, did you say? We eat samosas on pages on which the Geneva Convention is printed. Where is your family from?'

'We come from Lahore.' replied Suri.

'Where did your family live in Lahore?' asked the Pakistani.

'Mohalla Kuccha Chellan.'

'What did your father do?'

'He was a mathematics professor at Foreman Christian College.'

The Pakistani Major fixed him in a steady gaze and looked long at him. Suri felt the eyes bore into him hard. Had he said something inadvertently to offend the Pakistani, Suri wondered.

'Are you Professor Brij Mohan Suri's son?'

Suri gulped the hot Indian and Pakistani air. He suddenly felt thirsty. How the devil did this Pakistani Major know his father's name?

'You are two brothers and three sisters.' went on the Pakistani.

'Yes b…u…t…' stammered Suri.

'Your house was last but second in Gali Billa Singh.'

'Yes, that's right but…' Suri agreed in bewilderment.

The Pakistani officer got up from his steel chair and walked around the table. He took out an ivory-handled knife from his pocket, cut the rope, and set Suri's hands free.

'*Oye, kursi lao* (Hey, get a chair).' he shouted to an orderly.

'Sit down, Captain, and look at me.' insisted the Pakistani Major.

Suri sat down, dumbfounded at this sudden change in the demeanour of the Pakistani officer. Then the Major said, '*Saaley, tujhey yaad nahi mein tere ghar tuition padhne aata tha* (My dear fellow, don't you remember I used to come to study tuition at your house)? We used to be boys then. I am Rehman.'

The recall crashed on the baffles of his memory. Of course, he was the same boy who used to come on a black Raleigh bicycle and touch his father's feet every day.

'I am sorry it took me so long to recognise you,' said Suri wallowing in embarrassment.

'*Oye, chaa lao, chetti* (Hey, get tea, quick).' The Major's voice thundered at his orderly. He got up and came and embraced Suri. Then he said, 'Do you wish to see your old ancestral house?'

There were tears in Suri's eyes.

'Who doesn't wish to see one's birthplace again, Rehman?'

'Come then, let's not waste any time. Come with me to my tent.'

Suri followed the Pakistani Major to his tent.

'Wear my spare uniform. Take off your green uniform.'

Suri emerged from the tent clad in Rehman's khaki uniform. Rehman stepped forward and took off the Major's rank epaulettes from his own khaki shirt.

'Hope you won't mind being my batman for two hours.' said Rehman.

They climbed into the Major's jeep, and the jeep lurched towards the Lahore highway through the bald granary of Punjab. They entered Lahore, passed the Zamzama Canon at the Museum Circle, and then entered the old bustling quarter. The Major parked the jeep in front of Professor Suri's house and jangled the door chains. A boy opened the heavy wooden doors. A migrated family from India now lived in the old house. Suri touched the old familiar walls and the old wall niches which his sisters decorated with flowerpots. The house hadn't changed much. The same wooden pegs in the walls that hung clothes were still there. The inhabitants gave them *lassi sherbet* to drink in brass tumblers.

'Janab, *khana khaa ke jaiye* (Sir, please have food and go).' The Pakistanis were very hospitable.

'*Nahi, huzur, phir kabhi, shukriya* (No, Sir, maybe next time, thank you),' said Rehman.

It was late afternoon when they drove back to the Major's company. The company cook had laid out a feast in the water-sprinkled tent. Suri took out the two bottles of beer from his haversack that he was still carrying and luckily hadn't been relieved of.

'Here is to everlasting friendship.' They clinked the bottles.

A question troubled Suri's mind: What course of action would Major Rehman now take? Would he overlook the rules of his country for the sake of old ties and friendship? He asked himself what he would have done in his shoes if the position had been reversed. Suri was sure about his own convictions, that there was no question, the country would come above personal friendship.

'Now go and change into your own uniform,' said Major Rehman.

The sun hung low, like an orange plate in the clear silver sky. The earth breathed out the day's heat like heat coming out of an iron cooking vessel. The column of men walked through the gullies, and they came to where they had started.

'There is your *watan*, Suri. You are free now,' said Rehman pointing to the east. Suri and his men climbed a knoll. He looked back. There was no sign of the Pakistanis. Their jeep stood there, where they had left it, waiting for them to take them home.

The Distant Walls of School

It's raining military biographies these days. Every old soldier worth his millets is plying the quill. Whether it be about the arrival and departure of Ghazis, several stars of destiny, or the man behind the uniform and not inside it. It's a delightful time for chaps like me who love to read fauji blokes duelling with quill and ink. The hobby started after reading Subedar Sita Ram's biography, *From Sepoy to Subedar*, which is probably the first biography of an Indian Army personnel.

I was flipping through some General X's biography on the Kindle app out of idle curiosity. These days every man worth his jaggery is writing his military memoir or having a shadow writer do the job. How do you catch writing that has been done by a real fauji or a twenty-something writer-for-hire who is frequently tramping in and out of the dusty carpeted halls of Jaipur Lit Fest? My personal favourite for all time is not Cariappa, Thimmaya, Maneckshaw, etc., but a hill general who was a total antipode of the current genomes. Whereas some of today's X's only think of impoverishing the time-tested legacies of the organisation that has given them so much, General BC Joshi was probably the greatest visionary and an institution founder for us.

I don't believe in the hero cult. If we look into the personal lives of the poorest people around us, we find heroism beyond our pail of comprehension in their determination and daily battles with adversity and their unflagging will to overcome the odds of their lives. I check out books for the quality of writing, the ring of truth in the writing, and the chuckles I get when I detect something counterfeit. Hemingway had said that every decent writer must possess a built-in, shockproof, shit detector. Orwell wrote that no biography in which the author doesn't reveal his dark side and his own shortcomings is worth the paper on which it is written.

In the introduction to his autobiography, *Truth, Love & a Little Malice*, the wonderful doyen of Indian literature, Khushwant Singh, writes, 'I started on this autobiography with some trepidation... I am fast running out of writer's ink... I also have an enlarged prostate; at times, it produces illusions of youth in the form of massive erections in the mornings; at others, it does not give me enough time to undo my fly to urinate. I will have to get the prostate out soon, with it will go fake erections and youthful fantasies.' The inimitable Sardar wrote his biography when he was 87 years old and his candour and lifelong dedication to the literary craft and his literary output will not easily be surpassed.

What I recall from the early pages of the biography of X is that he mentions his childhood and gives the biographer some tidbits. His boyhood memories are given some play on the pages. He mentions a downhill run in a quest to catch the missed Army truck school bus in some hill station. The school bus was a modified 3-ton truck of the Army or something. Children loading up in trucks and going to school used to be the done thing, and I am glad X has mentioned this in his biography, for these days, the army cantonments have suddenly started vibrating with evangelical zeal of industrious military woodcutters searching for branches to cut on which they have been perched securely all their lives.

In my childhood, my mother withdrew me from a very good public school in Haryana against my father's wishes. I wasn't quite the star pupil of the class, and my marks on the report card were quite economical. She was convinced by the advice of the knowing neighbours, to whom she took my report card for perusal and comment, that Kendriya Vidyalaya education was far superior to my public school one. Having never gone to school herself, my mother wanted me to do better in life. We were in Simla, where my father had just come on posting from Nagaland when she got me home, and to my mother's bad luck, leave aside Kendriya Vidyalaya, no school in Simla Hills was willing to take me in. So, I got admission in a bleak house of a school straight out of a Charles Dickens novel – a *dingu* school in a poor man's house right above an apple orchard for children of very poor hill folks called *khadoos* (a native hillman). It was on the slope of Summerhill. If you looked up, you saw the looming masonry mountain of the grand Viceregal Cottage, the palace of the innumerable British Viceroys till 1947 and in whose grounds, I used to bunk and loaf around to my heart's content.

The school was not connected by road and was not on the list of registered and pedigreed schools in Simla. Some permanently constipated and haemorrhoiding station staff officers in the station headquarters refused me a school bus pass stating that there were no seats available in the truck buses that took kids to schools in Simla from Jutogh. Whenever I tried to get a lift in a school bus to get dropped at Bolileauganj on the road to Simla, I mostly got chucked out from the trucks. Sometimes, though, some kindly jawans did give me a lift. I was ten years old then. I would walk through the forested path for about two miles and reach my school. The Himachali hill kids found my raw Haryanvi accent rather forbidding, and teachers gawped with open mouths when I read out from the English reader. 'Sit down, boy. Which language are you speaking in?'

The fact that I was denied a school bus pass in an Army school bus so many years ago didn't rankle me all these years. In fact, I had almost forgotten the childhood injustice because my daily going and coming from school, mostly on foot, had opened the world around me, given me a good sensory memory, and a habit of not looking for help or favours from others.

I loved the railway track that I followed from Tutu to Summerhill to reach my school. The railway track was a shortcut, and I don't recall my mother or father ever getting the jitters about their boy walking all alone on the railway track to school. The power of the engine that came pulling the bogies was enthralling. I would often line up the tracks with ballast stones and stand and watch the engine's shining wheel crush the stones to powder. Many times, when I was crossing a tunnel, I heard a train coming on the track. I would run and stand in the walled recess in the dark tunnel and hear the deafening clamour of the passing train. I don't remember much of the education I received, but I remember the train, the trees, the flowers, the birds, the monkeys, and the people I watched.

Most khadoos always carried a Bittoo fountain pen with a round cap crown in their shirt or coat pockets. What did they have to write? But it was almost a religious symbol with the khadoos of Shimla – the omnipotent Bittoo pen in the breast pocket. It was, I think, something that made them appear respectable, like an Englishman wearing a tie. And respectable they were in my feral childhood. I never felt scared or intimidated, nor was I mistreated by anyone.

My daughter often teases me, 'Papa I wish I had legs like yours.' My younger sister used to say the same thing: '*Bhaiya*, you have legs like Steffi Graf.'

'I didn't have a school bus pass for three years when and I had to do a lot of hill-walking. You will never see a hill girl or a hill boy with weak legs. I became a khadoos for three years when I was very young.'

I had forgotten all about those vagabond years in Simla and all the loitering without intent that I used to do. Every summer, when the mountain oak used to burst into flowering, I would take my father's kitbag to collect *brass ke phool*, the pulpy red flowers that were used to make concentrated sherbet–something like the Roohafza sherbet. If I had been a regular school bus boy, I wouldn't have had the wonderous memories of freedom to roam around the hills of Simla. Many a time, I used to skip school and walk to the Mall Road and hang around that beautiful spot, hitching a ride back in some unsuspecting Shaktiman that was going towards Jutogh. It was very easy. You just had to stand at a steep uphill spot on the road from where you knew the truck would be grunting up the slope in low gear. Then you just had to run for five or ten yards behind it and leap and pull yourself up the tailboard. Unlike in the plains, in the hills, the driver would never peer back into the main body of the truck through the glass slats right behind his seat. When you reached your destination, you again waited for some spot where the truck would slow down, and you jumped out with a feeling of a small victory, having done a commando action and an adventure running amock in your stomach. The commando comics I used to read made me regard toughness and improvisation as premier qualities that a boy who wanted to join the army should inculcate.

Recently an NCO[1] posted to my unit came to me with a request. 'Sir, my wife travels 40 km a day to drop and pick up my two little kids to and from Army Public School. The military school bus stop is quite close to where my family lives in my hometown. My wife has gone to the Station Headquarters many a time to apply for the school bus passes but she has been told that there is no place in the buses from our stop.' He even gave me the name of the Station Staff Officer dealing with school buses. '*Aap inse baat kar lo. Afsar afsar ki sunta hai* (You speak to him. An officer listens to an officer).'

I asked a coursemate, who is a Brigadier posted in the same station, to help out in the matter. He remained too busy and probably it was too inconsequential a thing for his exalted highness to have gotten involved in. Anyhow, I summoned up my courage and decided to call the Station Staff Officer. His name looked helpful as he belonged to the same clan of homo sapiens as I do. I booked a call on the Army line and was fortunate that in the first shot itself, I was speaking to the Lord of the School Bus Passes. After pointing out to him that we belong to the same monkey tribe of homo sapiens, I requested two bus passes for my NCO's kids.

'It cannot be done,' was his cyclostyled answer, and he gave it with the practised ease and satisfactory pleasure of a man who has said 'no' to things all his life.

I made the mistake of saying, 'Sir, I am also a fauji kid. We have all travelled in truck school buses. So, why deny anyone who has legitimacy?'

'*Accha*, my father was in this cav,[2] and grandfather was also an officer in the same cav, and great grandfather was in the same cav, and his father was also in the same cav. From my

1. Non-commissioned Officer

2. cavalry regiment

wife's side, her father was in this cav, her father's father was also an officer in the same cav, and her father's father's father's father was also in the same cav. Do you want to hear more?'

I said, 'Sir, you have Missouris and Mississippis of blue blood flowing in your veins. Truly, you are the eighteenth generation of jaggery eater of fauj. What are two piddly bus passes for you? Sir, please be magnanimous.'

'It cannot be done for reasons you will not comprehend. Too much manpower is employed in school buses; these people are smart. They keep family in one place and keep availing school bus till their kids pass out.'

'Sir, what's wrong if they do so? Would you not have done the same if you were in his shoes?... You must be joking. We have Agniveers coming into the Army. Surely, they can be used as bus crew as they are good-for-nothing for four years.'

'It cannot be done.' he sang again.

'Sir, surely you remember the Chetwode motto? We are responsible for the welfare of our men. Arranging for sending their kids to school is the least and best welfare we can do for them.'

His majesty slammed the phone on me after saying, 'It cannot be done.'

If General BC Joshi had the same mingy spirit and depravity of vision, there would have been no Army schools in any cantonment and boys and girls would still be going in the same kind of Dickensian bleak house schools – the kind to which I went. But one thing is still good about the Army. We still have the same breed of constipated and haemorrhoiding station staff officers in charge of school bus passes who always say, 'It cannot be done.'

This Water Is Not for You

The regiment was out for winter war games and training manoeuvres in the Thar Desert. On one such morning, I was out on *shikaar* and shooting sand grouse in the dunes around Sheo in Barmer. The cool desert undulated all around, and the Mahindra jeep flew nicely over the sand in four-by-four gear.

After some time, Sowar Thomas, my driver, stopped the jeep and jumped out, saying that the jeep had overheated. He went and pulled up the bonnet hood. The jeep's engine was smelling of a heat-up. Thomas untied the canvas *chhagal* (water bag) from the jeep's bumper and poured water into the radiator. I tried starting the jeep, but the engine refused to cough up. We used up all the water, but the jeep would not start. I scanned the sandy horizon and saw a few huts about half a kilometre away.

'Take the chhagal and get some water from those huts.' I said to Thomas.

Thomas returned after almost 20 minutes and said that the occupants refused to give him water. I found it very strange that a soldier wearing the Army green uniform was refused water. What kind of people were they who couldn't part with two litres of water? I was a Captain and wore a three-starred cloth epaulette and felt that I would be able to draw out the water from them.

I said to Thomas, 'Come along. I will show you how to obtain water.'

We left the jeep with a pile of game birds, and I trotted off with Thomas into the dunes. The huts were thatched and conical-shaped. A six-foot tall Rajasthani with a pointy moustache stepped out when I shouted, '*Koi hai*?'

He stood and looked at me.

I said, 'You refused to give water to my man.'

'Yes, I did.'

'Do you have any water?'

'Yes, we do.'

'Do you want me to pay for the water?' I said, taking out my wallet.

'No, I don't need any money,' he said, showing me both his palms.

'Then can you fill up this chhagal for me?' I asked, extending the canvas water bag to him.

He jumped backwards as if I was trying to touch him with a live electric wire.

'I am not giving you a live snake! It's just a canvas water bottle, my good man.' I said, puzzled by the man's behaviour.

He explained, 'Sahib, we don't give water to anybody.' I was even more puzzled now. He had refused money, and he was refusing my request. I made another try. 'Look, brother, our jeep has heated up, and we have to pour water in its radiator to start it up. Our camp is ten miles away.'

The man said, 'Oh! You need water for the jeep. Then take it. My wife gets water from a *kooee* (well) very far off.'

He shouted, and a veiled woman, her silver amulets and anklets jingling, took the chhagal and came back and gave it to the man. He handed me the filled chhagal. I found his behaviour strange. I asked him why he had no problem giving water for the jeep but had refused it earlier.

'I am a *chamar*,[1] and nobody can drink my water. You will get polluted. That is why I refused you water.'

I was carrying my packed breakfast in a haversack. I told him to get his morning meal. He came out with a *baajra* roti, a chilli, a small onion, and *lahsun* chutney.

'You eat my food, and I will eat yours. We don't have any castes in the Indian Army.'

The tall man found it incredulous until he ate the omelette and toast, and I ate his baajra roti.

1. Indian leather craftsman

Meeting Khushwant Singh

Long ago I read a novella lying about in our house. It was Khushwant Singh's, *The Train to Pakistan*, which is one of the finest stories about India's partition. My love of Khushwant Singh's writing grew, and once I became an officer, I always got the *Hindustan Times* to read because it used to carry Khushwant Singh's column every Sunday – *With Malice Towards One and All.* I would take the newspaper cutting and file it in a separate file. My father was fond of telling me stories which he relished, and I heard many Khushwant Singh short stories from his mouth. Time flew. I also wanted to write stories, and the desire to meet the great Khushwant Singh grew and grew in me.

One day, I was passing by South Delhi and, just on a whim, I turned my car towards Sujan Singh Park. It was a winter evening, and a few men, who looked like servants and guards, were warming their hands over a fire as they sat around it on their haunches. I walked towards them and said that I wanted to meet Khushwant Singh.

One Garhwali-looking fellow looked up over his shoulders and said, 'You can't meet him just like that!'

'Look, brother, I am an Army officer and I have come from very far to meet him.'

'I work for Khushwant Singh. I will go and ask him if he will allow you to meet him.'

The hillman got up and went inside a ground-floor flat. He returned after five minutes, 'Do you have a visiting card? Sahib is asking for your card.'

I didn't have a visiting card, nor have I ever had one made. I took out my government-issued identity card, which I was carrying in my coat pocket to pass toll booths.

'This is the only card I have. Go and show him this.'

Again, the butler disappeared inside the house and came out after five minutes. This time, he said, 'You can come inside.'

I walked into a large drawing room at the far end of which sat Khushwant Singh with a glass full of very diluted whisky next to his chair. He had one leg resting on a cane *muddha*.[1] A black Mont Blanc ball pen peered out of the woollen Nehru jacket that he wore over his Punjabi kurta pyjama. A lady of younger years sat next to him, fawning and mothering him, 'Khushwant, you must not do this. Oh, Khushwant! How have you been? Oh, Khushwant! How nice to meet you again.'

Then this darkish woman looked at me from my thick black mop of hair down to my toes and, curling up her nose, said to me, 'Who are you, and why do you come here to disturb this poor old man? What businesses have you here? Why don't you leave and let him be?'

I just stood stunned by the hostile reception of the woman. I turned into a marble statue, and when I regained my composure, I turned to leave, muttering, 'I am sorry. I have made a mistake. I shouldn't have come.'

I had taken two steps towards the door when I heard,

---

1. Indian reed stool

'Wahida, he has come to my doorstep, I can't turn him away just like that. Come, Major, sit next to me. Care to have a drink? There is the bar; pour yourself a drink.'

I went and sat next to him and saw that he had been reading a book written in Urdu. I declined to have a drink.

'Where are you posted these days?' he asked.

'Sir, I am in Kashmir.'

'Beautiful spot.'

'Yes, Sir. Sir, what have you been reading? I am very fond of your writing.'

'This is the Diwan of Ghalib. I quite love Ghalib. I will recite a poem of his.'

Then Khushwant Singh started reciting yards and yards of Ghalib from his copious memory.

Soon it was time for me to leave.

'Go and pick up any book from that pile of books lying there.'

I found a nice book of poems which he autographed for me and then I thanked him and left.

During the Khalistani movement of the 1980s, Khushwant Singh was a very vocal critic of the Khalistani leaders. Sikhs all over the world got annoyed at him and started sending him letters from all over the world, filled with the choicest Indian and Punjabi *gaalis*.[2] Sikhs also started stopping him if they saw him walking anywhere to do *gaali-galoch* on him.

He recounted in an article: 'One classic letter was sent to me by a Sikh from Canada. The letter was written in Gurmukhi script. Only on the envelope, where the address is to be written, were four words in English: Bastard Khushwant Singh, India.

'This letter was posted from Canada, and the efficiency of the Indian Postal Services astonished me. In a country with a population of 125 crore, they were able to locate the "bastard" and deliver the letter to me.'

2. abuses

Officers and Gentlemen

The Army soldiers were marching with stiff legs in new uniforms, and the senior officers were laying wreaths on stone memorials. The bugle blew and stilled the air. Everybody raised their arms in salute. Another fifteenth of August was here. The photographers aimed their cameras and clicked photos. Remembrance was almost over.

The flowers stay for a day or two on the stone slabs, doing their work above and beyond the call of duty. The engraved names on the walls look onto the flowers; the people have all gone. Flowers live after they are cut, beautiful even in death.

The stylish and fad-crazed early morning runners, with smartwatches and mobile phones glued onto their arms, are already thinking of running for the next ceremonial marathon – the next event of photos and attention appetite. 'Hey, buddy, I ran today. The Fifteenth August Memorial half marathon. Fifteenth August is over, but man, I ran. Lots of photos. Good fun and time to put new DP[1] and new status.' But the names on the stones on the wall have their own story, don't they?

My brother was so handsome—a better man than I could ever imagine being. When he laughed, the sun would be envious of the happiness that shone on his face. He flew fighter aircraft. I wanted to be a fighter pilot just like him and join the 101 Squadron—his squadron.

The year was 1971 and I was in senior school. My brother, Vijay, had qualified the tests to fly both the MiG-21 as well as Sukhoi 7 fighter aircraft. His squadron, the 101 Squadron, had converted from Hunter aircraft to Sukhoi 7s. The choice was for him to join a new squadron of MiG-21s or remain with his old squadron and fly the slower and older Sukhoi 7 fighter.

That summer, I, too, got selected for the National Defence Academy's 45th Course. Delhi was burning hot in the heat of June. The loo blew furiously on the plains. The dry pods on the *sheesham* trees beat their own summer music in the hot wind. I would be joining NDA soon and then join my brother's squadron.

That summer, my brother was on leave in Delhi. After clearing the services selection board interview, I, too, went to Delhi for my Air Force medical fitness tests. I had been reading up and talking about aeroplanes all my boyhood years. My brother made his choice.

'There is not the same fun in flying a Sukhoi 7 as there is in flying a MiG 21. The Sukhoi 7 is a slower fighter bomber of an earlier type. The MiG 21 is a better aircraft. But I have no regrets; I want to stay with my friends and my own squadron. The MiG, no doubt, is a better bird, but since 101 is converting from Hunters to Sukhois, I have decided not to join the new MiG aircraft squadron. I will stay with my old squadron.'

---

1. display picture

His squadron was like a family to him. They had a pilot whom they called Lambretta. He was a couple of years senior to my brother. He was married to an extraordinarily beautiful lady. Soon after their wedding, the Lambrettas had a daughter. Later, the husband and wife started having differences. They had another daughter. Then the family split and the lady moved to Delhi with her daughters from that air force base.

I had come to Delhi for my medicals. My brother, then, was staying in a flat at Officer's Enclave near Dhaula Kuan. Although I was accommodated for medicals in the Air Force hostel, I used to spend all my spare time at my brother's flat. Many of my cousins had also come over during their summer holidays, and I remember us all having a lot of fun together.

My brother came along with me for the medical tests. His ex-squadron doctor was a medical examiner in the medical establishment. He urged the doctor. 'Sir, he is my kid brother, and he has cleared NDA. He has to come to 101 Squadron. You have been our old squadron doctor. Please, clear him, Sir. He will fly as my wingman in 101 Squadron one day.'

Around that time, one day I was at home with a lot of my younger cousins in the house. Brother had gone out somewhere. He used to have a blue-coloured Standard Herald car then. He had switched from his Java motorcycle to this car. At about 10 a.m., the bell rang. I went to open the door. As soon as I opened it, I saw a stunningly beautiful woman standing there. I rubbed my eyes and looked at her again. I had never seen anyone so gorgeous in my life. Then I thought that she must be my brother's girlfriend.

'Is Flight Lieutenant Vijay in?' she asked in a nice voice.

I said he had gone out for a while, but would she please come in and wait for him?

She said, 'No, I will have to go. The autorickshaw is waiting for me downstairs. I had just come to say hello to Vijay.'

She told me her name and went away. I have forgotten what her name was. I was tickled by the thought of meeting my brother's girlfriend just by chance. My younger cousins were all tender-aged *bhondus*.[2] I thought I would tease my brother about his girlfriend once he returned. Now that I had discovered his secret, I waited anxiously, barely able to control my excitement. Soon I heard his foot fall on the stone stairs. He entered, and I started to tease him, winking and making eyes at him.

'What is this big brother? *Aap to chupey rustum ho* (You're quite the hidden talent). *Bataya tak nahi* (You didn't even reveal it). Salim and Anarkali full on and nobody in the family knows.'

My brother was confused seeing my behaviour.

'Who had come? Describe her,' he asked.

'Brother, really! You do good acting.'

'Shut up and describe her.'

I described her and said some very filmy things about her and my brother. The next thing I felt was an arm flying and a tight slap on my cheek.

'Shut your mouth, you clueless idiot.'

'Do you know who you are talking about? She is the wife of a brother officer. And you are talking a load of rubbish about her. What *badtameezi*!'[3]

'I didn't know that. I am very sorry, brother,' I replied sheepishly rubbing my burning cheek.

'Do you know she must have had her two little girls with her in that auto? She is the wife of a brother officer of my squadron, and they are separated for the time being. There are four of us young officers of our squadron who pool in our flying pay and send her the money every month.'

---

2. stupid

3. unmannerly

I felt like an utter fool, and I felt sad for the lady with her two little girls, who had been left by her husband to fend for herself.

'Young brother, you have a life lying ahead of you. Never, never look at any lady with a bad eye. When I have to get married you will be the first one to know.'

I had learnt my lesson – never talk loose about a lady.

My brother died in the skies over the Battle of Chambb during the December 1971 war with Pakistan. He won a Vir Chakra for his actions. I could not join the Air Force. I became an Army doctor instead.

When I retired, I had to go to Jorhat for some urgent work. I boarded a northeast flight from Calcutta. A young lady came and sat down in the seat next to mine. I started talking to her. She must have been a college-going kid.

'*Beta*, where are you travelling to in the northeast?' I asked her.

'Uncle, my father is the Air Officer Commanding in Tezpur. I am visiting my father.'

I asked her what her father's name was.

She said, 'Sir, he is Air Commodore Lambretta.'

'Is he ex-101 Squadron?'

'How do you know, Sir? Yes, he has served in 101 Squadron.'

I said, '*Beta, woh kahani aap ko kya batau* (Child, what do I tell you about that tale)? It is an old tale. Is your mother there with your father?'

She said, 'Yes.'

'She is living with your father now.'

She said, 'Yes, Sir. But why do you ask, Sir? Was she ever living away from my father?'

I said, 'No, indeed not. I didn't mean it that way. Please pay my respect to your mother and tell her that you met Flight Lieutenant Vijay's younger brother. I think it will make her happy.'

The Reader

He entered the bookshop, which was almost hidden in the corner of the building. The building was a government-run art centre and always had sprawling exhibitions going on in its various pavilions.

Lines of school children walked past the stalls, minded by their teachers, and there was also the Army Wives Welfare Association Literary Festival going on. Many analyses-paralysis self-important generals and brigadiers sat there in the courtyard on red stone stairs, trying to look absorbed and dutifully literary because their wives were trying to look literarily bent because their bosses' wives had been throwing around names of books they were currently reading. The thing he felt was that the army's professional requirements were met by other phenomena like zero error and DS solutions and rules and regulations for everything. So much of regulations, rules, and SOPs[1] were rammed down right from a person's throat to the big toe that

1. standard operating procedures

everybody had atrophied and SOP-ified. There would always be a contradiction to everything literary in the Services.

He looked at the schoolchildren and felt a tremor of irony pass through his senses when he saw that all the children were from the local Army Public School. He, too, had studied in an Army Public School. The children were wearing the same silver and red ties. Their ties hung loose from the collars just like his had done – like a formality. But he had been fastidious about his appearance. He went to the thief's market under the walls of the Red Fort to buy his shirts for school. What an age is teenage when your looks, hairstyle, and fashion sense overpower you.

He remembered that day in his eleventh class after the two months of summer holidays when the very attractive English teacher had asked the class, 'What did you read in your two months' summer vacations?' He was sitting on the last desk, and he had raised his hand. No other hand went up – he had been the only one. The attractive teacher's eyes were fixed on him. He froze in self-consciousness as if he were a wild hare caught in a car's light.

'What did you read?' She asked, smiling condescendingly as if she caught him overselling himself for attention. After all, he had never before opened his mouth in the English class and always sat on the last bench.

He got up. She saw that he was very precocious, and his cheeks were already red. He had folded his shirt sleeves over his elbows, and she thought that he was good-looking, but he looked painfully shy to the point of appearing frozen. His large black eyes almost covered all the white of his eyes.

'Ma'am, I read *The Count of Monte Cristo* by Alexandre Dumas, *A Tale of Two Cities* and *Nicholas Nickleby* by Dickens, and *The Three Musketeers* by Alexandre Dumas.'

'Oh, really?' She found it hard to believe.

'Ma'am.'

'Can you narrate the story of *The Count of Monte Cristo*?'

'Ma'am, I think I can.' he replied

Everyone looked at him in disbelief. Most so the teacher. They expected him to make a fool of himself, and they would laugh and make fun of him.

He spoke for 40 minutes, and all 50 faces, including the teacher's, had listened to his narration without once interrupting.

The bell rang, and the teacher got up, looking back over her shoulders as she went out. She was very beautiful, he thought. He had secretly started longing for his teacher.

His best friend in the class came and said, 'Dude, that was some telling of the story you did. Why didn't you ever tell me that you read?'

He believed that reading and love are best done in absolute secrecy and sacredness. But his friend would have laughed at him if he had told him as much.

He heard some writers speak, had gotten bored and strolled about. That's when he found the bookshop.

'I could talk better than them about the subject of writing stories,' he felt. But again, he felt he could never speak about reading and writing in front of anyone. He disliked the word 'writer'. He loved to think of himself as a maker of something. A mere workman. Like a carpenter making things out of wood, he liked making things out of words, and that's all there was to it, he told himself. A carpenter working with words – that is the feeling he honoured inside himself. But again, he could never tell that to anyone.

'How may I help you?' he heard a voice while his mind had been roaming the long road of memory. Nobody was visible inside the bookshop as he had swung the glass door. He had thought that the shop was empty. The voice repeated the inquiry. This time he felt the voice was sterner.

The stranger who had entered the bookshop didn't look like the book-reading sort. She looked up from the corner where she was reading a book. She was small, like a sparrow.

The visitor was wearing jeans with a hole in the thigh. She was aware of these kinds – they were loafers who came out of curiosity to look at the books. And where they saw a young girl, there they went to ogle at her. She had no patience for these sorts of illiterate literates.

She sat behind the glowing screen of her computer, observing the man who looked like a fauji. There was some fauji literary show going on in the art centre, she knew. She knew what the men came looking for in her bookshop – just sleaze. She had no books or magazines with models or sugar candies.

She became curious, curious to see what this man would pick first. She was aware of the contents of each section, book, and magazine in her bookshop. Every morning, she dusted and arranged the bookshelves herself, like a woman keeping her jewellery.

The man seemed flustered as if he had stepped into an unfamiliar place, or, at least, that is what she thought. On the other hand, she felt her hallowed space invaded by an alien – a man in torn jeans and an old, faded cotton T-shirt.

'Yes, what do you want?' she asked. Her words sounded like a lash from a whip.

The man was startled by the menace, and he turned his head with a jerk towards the sound and saw her. A pinched headmistress-like face, she glared at him like an angry squirrel who felt someone had come to snatch her chestnut. He became aware that he didn't look educated nor like a good customer, nor moneyed, therefore the hostility.

'I was wondering if you would allow me to trespass in your bookshop for a while. I might just find a book I would like to buy,' he answered in a soft and sweet voice.

She was so surprised. Hostility turned into cordiality in the passage of a second.

'Yeah, sure,' she said, motioning with her right hand towards the bookshelves. She was now sweet and charming. After a while, she asked him, 'Are you looking for Chetan Bhagat by any chance?'

The man was amused. The man looked at her contemplatively and answered, 'I was rather hoping. I am a huge fan of Chetan Bhagat.'

'Ahh! I see,' she said snootily as if the discovery and confirmation had clicked into the proper slot in her mind.

'I don't keep any Chetan Bhagat books in my bookshop. He is infra dig,' she spoke, relishing a cold triumph over him.

She saw that he had picked up a book in his hands. He was listening intently to the loud clucking of a pigeon that was trying to lay an egg in the ventilator of the bookshop. The neck of the pigeon was swelling and falling with each sonorous note. He stood and read from the book, intermittently taking his eyes up to the ventilator.

'That book in your hands. It is a fabulous book,' she said.

It was a book on the interpretation of Greek myths by Robert Graves. The man had read about Robert Graves, one of the great English poets of the First World War, along with Wilfred Owen and Siegfried Sassoon. He had been trying to recollect a poem by Graves as he looked up at the noisy bird. And he remembered the lines about the passage of seasons. Graves had said, 'I watched the seasons passing slow, so slow in the fields between La Bassée and Bethune; primroses and the first warm day of spring.' La Bassee, he noted from memory, was also the 5 Sikh Battalion's battle honour. They celebrated La Bassee Day.

During the war, Graves had been ripped in the chest with a shell fragment that went through the lungs. He was expected to die, and the battalion clerk officially reported him as having died of wounds. He survived and went on to live till 90. He had read Robert Graves. He had also known the movie called *Benediction* on another World War One poet – Seigfried Sassoon – by some wizard movie director.

'Who is this author, Robert Graves?' he asked the prim girl, throwing a bait to her. It remained to be seen how she would swallow it.

She pinned him down with a superior gaze.

'Marvellous book. I have read the whole book. I can highly recommend it. It's a lovely book.'

'Oh,' he exclaimed. 'Was he a poet too? Has he written any poems – this author, Robert Graves?'

She eyed him from the rim of her tortoise-shell glasses like a class teacher who feels annoyed by an unexpected question. Some young girls, he had noticed, wore extra-large reading glasses. This one was wearing a bead necklace and a cotton kurta. She wasn't beautiful by his idea of beauty, but she was competent and good-looking. He thought that he would not mind doing her job as a bookshop minder. When he was in a bookshop, he missed following the alternate life he fantasised about. He dreamt that he would write many things and his books would be there on bookshelves even 100 years after his death. Like this book on Greek mythology by Robert Graves. He was an army officer, but he knew he was a different sort of army officer because he had read a lot of work written by people who had army experience. Leo Tolstoy and Hemingway had army experience too. He wondered if anybody could write without having been a soldier. But India was different. Here soldiers never read and never wrote anything of worth or value. The white man of the West was different.

He heard the girl's voice break his reverie. 'No other. Graves only wrote one book, and you are holding it in your hands.

It is a bestseller.' After a pause, she added, 'I give my special customers a ten per cent discount.'

'I see. That is very kind of you,' he said as he replaced the book on the shelf.

He left without buying any books. The girl shrugged and returned to reading *Fifty Shades of Grey*, which she had been reading when he had entered the bookshop. He had read somewhere that *Fifty Shades of Grey* was being devoured by women all over the globe.

Diwali Cess

A group of Army officers was keeping their used plates and cups on a side table after a tea-ing out for a brother officer.

One of their colleagues had got his posting to Leikabali. He had the Punjabi habit of boasting and had been boasting for the past almost two months – '*Fauj* never sends me on a posting. I choose a posting. I put my index finger on a good city, and then I go there. Nobody's pop has the power to deny me choice posting.'

Well, we had just had the poor fellow's farewell tea. He had been posted to one of those mysterious, unpronounceable places across the Kachin hills and the Brahmaputra. Ultimately, the MS Branch is like Muhammad Ali, dealing with lightweight officers. We had never heard the place's name! People there still wore animal skin skirts! Such places exist only for the gentlemen of the Indian Army to enjoy or suffer, depending on one's attitude.

'*Koi gall nahi. Agli posting to me Patiala ki hi loonga* (Never mind, I will take the next posting of my choice, and that will be Patiala),' he said with the dust of vanity scattering around him.

As soon as he left, our boss rounded us up and said, 'Gentlemen, tomorrow evening is the customary pre-Diwali party at the General's house. Please be there with your better halves. No one is to be missing. You have no choice in this matter. This is a compulsory party.' He concluded like a judge, sounding the gavel before announcing a particularly harsh punishment.

Someone said that he had secretly started polishing his general's badges of rank the day he got his present rank and was working for yet another gleaming nine-pointer. I laughed. It sounded far-fetched. Who bothers with ACRs[1] so much?

But forgive me for digressing from the story.

Diwali is a time like no other. We had started playing *teen patti* a week prior. We drank like thirsty pilgrims and spent the days reeking like a distillery.

'*Nahi yaar*. I will be missing tonight. We have to attend that General's party. By order. *Baa hukum*.' I told my friend.

He advised, '*Arrey kuch nahi hota* (Oh, nothing happens). Make some *aisa waisa* excuse and bunk it.'

I have some qualms in these sorts of matters. I dislike discourtesy and under-handedness. Hadn't the Brigadier said that it was a compulsory party and that we must be proper OG and obedient chaps and follow orders masked as requests.

The Edwardian bungalow on the Mall Road was lit like the White House. Over the emerald-green painted pediment was a beautiful crest of horses. Below it were three words of a code that said 'Loyal unto Death'.

Soft light spilt onto manicured lawns out of the gracefully arched verandas. A tablet read that the house was built for an amount of ₹14,500 in 1920.

They stood welcoming the mass of officers jamming the portico of the fine old bungalow. Our boss was mouthing

1. Annual Confidential Report

best wishes and extending packets of Diwali *nazraana* to the General. We had all contributed money for the procurement of these costly ambassadorial presents, which our Commandant was now presenting to the senior officer.

My lady and I were a trifle late. We slipped in quietly into the tail end of the herd of guests. They shuffled onward on slow feet. It felt like a reception of an Indian *baraat*. Soon a batman of the household thrust a carton of *barfi* in front of me. I picked a piece and mumbled my best Diwali wishes to the host. He smiled the smile that said he was clearly in no need of the best wishes of humbletons like me, or was it just my overactive imagination?

A waiter came and asked about my drink. I stood holding a glass of whisky, chatting to an officer about the trend doing the rounds in appointment houses. The previous resident's names were marked on a board of occupancy on the veranda of the bungalow. The General approached us. He wore a teal-coloured *sadri*[2] over a long Mughal kurta. He held a cut glass of pomegranate juice. He noticed my glass and said, 'Your glass is empty. It's a sacrilege. You can't nurse an empty glass in my party. Waiter, get this officer a refill, *ekdum abhi*.'

What a fine host. What a superlative General. I winced at the thought of the amount of badmouthing that we do of our seniors on social media groups and in person. Really, we junior officers were a nasty lot, always digging for dirt and salacious gossip like ferrets about our seniors. Pangs of contrition and remorse started banging in the chambers of my heart.

I felt like fasting and doing *paschyaatap*[3] like the *rishis* and *munis*[4] of yore. I wanted to purify my soul of my previous sins

2. Nehru Jacket

3. repentance

4. sages

of thinking lowly of my superiors. I wanted to burn my tongue that had sometimes called them freeloaders and their behaviour as *ghatiya*[5] behaviour unbecoming of an army officer.

The General moved to the next cluster of guests. 'Come on folks, enjoy yourself. You are at my house. Feel free.' I heard him say in jolly tones with warm hospitality.

The General's efficient staff officer was soon seen whispering to guests to start eating and clear off by 9 p.m. I picked up my plate and was putting a second spoon of *keema* in my mouth when the General walked up to me. 'How's the food?'

'Sir, it's very good.'

'Eat! Eat to your fill!' he said.

At this point, I thought the General was trying to cover up a smirk, or was it my imagination that he seemed to be gloating at the contents of my plate?

'Come on, have some more,' he said with eyes that gleamed with sincere and wholesome hospitality. I wondered whether the expression could be called a smile. He smiled strangely, or was it my suspicious imagination? Anyhow, he jumped up a few notches in my esteem that evening. It really impressed me that such philanthropic senior officers still existed. I always like to believe that the best in a person is natural and genuine. He had personally talked to me twice.

'What a fine host,' I said to my wife on our way out. The honest glow of admiration shone brightly in my eyes. I felt the world was a good place, and I felt contempt for the doubting Thomases of the world who only searched for trickery and deceit in everyone's character. Soon, we had to watch out and jump up to the footpath to avoid Oriflamed staff cars and other cavalcades of select guests of the General for whom we had been corraled out in a hurried manner.

---

5. lowly

Anyhow, Diwali was over. I was sitting at my office desk when the phone rang on the subsequent day. '*Saabji*, I am the Mess Havildar Satwant speaking.'

'Yes, Satwant,' I answered, recognising his voice.

'*Saabji*, baby had not come to General Saab's Diwali party?'

'No, Satwant, my daughter hadn't attended the fine party.'

I was touched by Mess Havildar's concern. The Indian Army is like a family. Even today, the men care for their officers and officers for their men. What a fine Mess Havildar—even among the crowd, he noticed that my daughter was missing. I was so touched that I was almost willing to forgive him the usual accusations that my wife levied on him after perusing my monthly mess bill. '*Woh, tumhara* Sardarji Mess Havildar – *poora ka poora chor hai* (Your Sardarji Mess Havildar – he's entirely a thief). He is shamelessly making money by overcharging officers.'

'*Ji, Saabji.*'

He was about to disconnect when doubt flickered in my thoughts.

'Say, Satwant, why did you ask about my daughter?'

'Oh, *Saabji, mein General saab ki party ke expenditure ki baat kar raha tha* (Oh, Sir, I was talking about the expenses for the General's party). I have been ordered to distribute the party expenditure equally to all officers.'

I didn't speak for a while.

'How much will it be per officer?'

'*Saabji, zyada nahi. Yahi koi do hazaar rupiya.* (Sir, not much. Just around two thousand Rupees.)'

'*Acha, Saabji, sat sri kaal. Apke mess bill me daal diya hai.* (Okay, Sir, goodbye. I have added it to your mess bill.)'

But hadn't we been invited as guests? Since when have officers started inviting guests to their houses and sending them a hospitality/mess bill the next day? I scratched my head. If there was such a rule or practice, I wasn't aware.

In the haze of this surprise, I remembered the gimlet eyes of the General appraising my empty whiskey glass.

There was a flashback. 'Waiter, *Sahib ka glass khaali hai. Sahib ka drinks lao*.' 'Young man, how is the keema?' The warm memory of the evening returned. I laughed and laughed.

Disclaimer: This is a work of fiction. Any resemblance to events, places, or characters is entirely coincidental.

Castrol Problem

The three *sardar* soldiers and one *monaa* soldier crossed me like a bunch of faujis who have hastily jumped out of Auchinleck Araamgaah at the Old Delhi Railway Station and are running to catch the departing Punjab Mail. Always in a tearing hurry, straining hard, running hard. They came out running every evening at dusk when the sun was about to dip.

They ran in combat dress, their boots grating on the hard black road. They ran in a tight pack. Sometimes, I saw them in the distance, like dancing shadows in the night. Noticing them became a habit. The days on which I didn't see them, I felt a pang of disappointment. 'Why haven't the night runners come today?'

The four of them usually came just after dusk, when the night was opening its eyelids. They did a swift five kilometres run around the peripheral road and disappeared back into the black door of the night.

It appeared as if the three sardars were running with a quarter-guard prisoner. One sardar ran behind the monaa, one on his left and one on his right. Being in combat trousers and combat T-shirts, they were not clearly visible, and I was often surprised when I saw them appear out of nowhere like ghosts.

The monaa *sipahi* held his hands behind his back, like in a *vishraam*[1] position, his hands tied, with the three sardar guards around him. I thought that this remarkable old-school infantry battalion sent its quarter-guard prisoner for a five-kilometre run every evening, and the prisoner seemed to willingly run with his hands tied behind his back. I had never seen such a cooperative prisoner. Many times, I wondered what his offence could have been.

The sardars used to wish me *Sat Sri Akal* and run past me. They were swift runners, and their running speed was much better than mine. A few times, I foolishly tried to match strides with them but soon gave up. They were much faster than me.

Sometimes I crossed the running squads of a special forces battalion in the station also. Quite a few of them kept beards, and they ran with a small pack full of gravel. Some of these fellows were not prone to say Jai Hind to anybody. They jogged on with dour faces, quietly absorbing the wear that comes from regularly running endless miles with leaden weights on their backs. They had to pass their tough fitness tests.

One day, I was surprised by a para trooper running in a long line of troopers on an endurance run. When he crossed me, he said a cheerful Jai Hind.

After he had crossed me, I said loudly, '*Rukko* (Stop).'

He was running with another man, and both of them stopped and turned back to face me. He had a sudden fear on his face as if he had done something wrong. He said to me, 'Sir, *koi galti hui* (Sir, have I made any mistake)?'

I smiled at him and said, 'At least 50 men of your battalion have crossed me, and you are the only one who wished me Jai

1. stand-at-ease position

Hind. I just wanted to tell you that you are exceptional. The rest of them don't seem to have air left in their tyres.'

He was very happy, and he smiled and trotted away. He was one tail-up soldier in a crowd of tail-downs.

Yet, the night runners were the group I looked forward to crossing every evening. I had developed a fondness for them. They ran as if they were running from choice rather than by order. They were from a good battalion – one could make out the morale and quality of soldiers from a mile. It was the cheerfulness, thoroughness, and easy courtesy with which soldiers of their battalion handled the affairs of the main gate of the cantonment and all other duties.

The main gates of the military station were a beehive of activities. There were dozens of faceless, poor labourers that poured in to work on MES construction sites, carrying their two *katoris* (bowls) – stainless steel tiffin boxes – and their toddlers. Endless vehicles went in and out, and the soldiers at the gate had to check everybody. The labourers came in the mornings, both men and women. The women with silver *payals* on their ankles and *bicchuas* on their toes walked lightly with their infants held in the saddle of their waistline. They toiled throughout the day's heat.

There used to be a young female labourer whom I had seen when I had come on posting. I walk a lot, and one day, I stopped to watch a young woman swinging the pickaxe in a long ditch that she was digging next to a road to lay some underground cables. She was sparkling with youth. She had a beauty that even the digging she was doing only elevated. I was wondering how, with such a slight body and such narrow elbows, she was able to do the back-breaking work. The anklets on her ankles, the nose pin, the necklace of silver rupee coins, and the myriad tattoos on her face and the pickaxe – I thought it was all wrong.

She used to work with two extremely thin, whippet-like young men who had very narrow skeletons and were naturally thin. In the initial days, she used to smile and joke, and they would be seen taking turns digging, resting in the shade, and drinking water from a two-litre Coca-Cola plastic bottle. Many times, I saw the two boys stop digging and take out small sachets of *gutkha*.[2] They would tear a pouch, pour the contents into their mouths, throw away the pouch, and resume digging. The girl used to wear a long blue skirt and a short shirt that left her belly visible. She had a narrow belly. They were all from a narrowly built tribe of people.

She had an *odhni* or a *chunni* hanging from her head over her back. She always seemed to be doing more work than the two young men who ate gutkha all the time. She was an unusual labourer, and God had given her an attractive face, fair skin, and light hair. The manual labour made her cheeks red, and she was not very tall – maybe just an inch or two above five feet. She had a softly rounded lower belly that curved outwards a bit. I couldn't help thinking that women have a birthright to beauty and their form has sovereignty that cannot be destroyed by digging ditches under the hot Rajasthani sun.

Of and on, I would see this triumvirate of the pickaxe and hoe, working around MES projects, sometimes constructing a fence around a transformer, sometimes breaking feeble cement plaster of boundary walls with hammers. In between, I once saw the beautiful labourer had also started eating Gutkha. I wondered for how long her beauty would last because I estimated her age to be about eighteen or nineteen years.

As the months dragged on, I lost sight of this trio, and I thought they might have sought work with some other contractor and migrated. Almost a year passed, and then the second year.

2. a chewing tobacco product

One day, when I was cycling back through the main gate of the cantonment, I crossed a group of labourers exiting, and my eyes fell upon a woman walking in a long skirt and a choli, covered in dust, her skin dry and sunburnt. She still wore a long skirt, but her whole aspect was that of a 40-year-old person. The grace of limbs and the youthful walk had deserted her, and she looked like an old woman. It was my once-charming labourer whom I was seeing, now almost an unrecognisable, worn-out woman. I thought her grace in the movement of her pickaxe-swinging shoulders was like notes of music the first time I had seen her.

The much over-geared sentries of the gate, with plastic elbow and knee shields, high boots, a scarf around their neck, and sometimes black goggles, appeared like Hollywood movie soldiers. The old DSC[3] soldiers who man the couriers counter at the main gate are earthy men. Devoid of ornaments, they sit at their plastic table with a ball pen and spectacle case, patiently making parcel entries in the registers. Their good old black bicycles with sturdy carriers are kept parked next to the wall, bearing the name, number, and rank of the owner. They are dozy and have the bored, I-have-seen-it-all look of old soldiers who take the DSC's shilling to see their children through college and getting degrees. Having been buffeted in all corners of India for lack of employment, they finally head towards the spice city of Cannanore.

It happened that the shadowy runners stopped crossing me after a while, and I thought that the prisoner's quarter-guard imprisonment term must have gotten over. It couldn't go beyond 28 days. I started missing the 'runners of the dusk'. The road lay black and silver with not a soul was on it. The tiny spatula-like lights that the MES had put on the street light poles gave out

3. Defence Security Corps

the same hydrogen light that Kia and BMW car lights give – kind of blinding torture for the eyes, never to be looked at.

The thin gardener boy, who watered the grassy sprawl of the polo fields around which the polo field ran, lugging black water sprinkler pipes, had also stopped running after the army enrolment system changed. I was walking down the road, thinking about the feasibility of buying a new pair of walking shoes. The sole of my shoes had worn out, even tiny pebbles pricked the skin now. I thought, what's the point of wasting money? I would buy a cheap pair from the CSD canteen. The sitting committee of ways and means in my mind, which was discussing household expenses, was disturbed by the sight of something moving on the road in the far distance. Could it be the blue bulls that were numerous in this area, or could it be somebody like me, fond of walking in the dark?

The scrape and rub of hard boots on the road became audible before the owners of the noise became visible in the darkness. The bobbing turbans looked like the heads of a blue bull in the dark until they came closer. The sardars were again out running and tucked between them was a crewcut monaa! His hands were still implacably tied behind his back. I shouted and stopped them after they had crossed me.

They stopped.

'Where have you people been for so long? I am seeing you after a long time.' I was glad to see them.

'*Sahabji*, our company had gone out of station for training,' said one of the sardars.

I ran my eyes over the perspiring monaa soldier whose hands were behind his back.

'Has his 28 days rigorous imprisonment not gotten over yet?' I said, pointing my finger at the monaa.

The monaa looked at the sardars, and one of the sardars looked at me.

'Sir, I have not understood what you are saying.'

I said, 'Isn't this man a prisoner? His hands are tied behind his back. Tell me, what was his offence?'

Suddenly the monaa soldier, who was standing with his hands stuck behind his back, loosened his arms, freed them, and brought them forward. I was quite taken aback. It seemed his hands were not tied after all.

'Why do you take out this person for a run every night?' I asked.

The group stood quietly, and I probed on.

'Why do you people come out for a run after dark? Don't you have PT and games parades in your unit?'

'Sir, this person has a high Castrol problem,' one of them replied.

'What is a high Castrol problem?' I asked, uncomprehending.

'Sir, Castrol problem keeps coming in my blood report during my medical examination,' said the crewcut man, helpfully.

'Oh, I see, okay.' A realisation came upon me. This man had high blood cholesterol levels.

I was still confused about the necessity of the monaa soldier running with his hands stuck behind his back, like a man with amputated arms. 'But, why do you always run in a vishram position?'

'Sir, if you run in a vishram position, the Castrol problem finishes.' He had the ring of a *mandir* bell conviction in his voice.

'Who told you so?' I asked him gently.

'It's an old tradition of our battalion. It is a remedy passed down by our seniors. We all run like this when we get a Castrol problem, and the Castrol goes away.'

Give Me Your Black Scarf

We all knew the war would come. It was only a matter of days, maybe a few weeks at most. We were at Chambb, which is today occupied by Pakistan. It seems so absurd that we should have lost this piece of India to Pakistan. This is my story to tell, and I must tell it to someone. In a way, it is also the story of two friends who found themselves on the same battlefield in those few fateful days.

We were sitting in his company-defended locality at Point 303 when Major Pannu, the infantry Company Commander looked at the black scarf that I was wearing around my neck in my uniform and said to me, 'Iesh, you give me your black armoured corps scarf. It's looking smart, and I want to wear it.'

He was fond of scarves, and he used to always dress up smartly.

'What will I wear then?' I said to him.

He was not one to lack a solution for anything.

He was a Sikh, and he took off the olive green turban that he was wearing on his head.

'Here is my infantry green turban, you can make a scarf for yourself from it.'

I took off my black scarf and gave it to Major Pannu. We had been coursemates at NDA, and here we were, once again thrown together in Chambb, where his battalion was deployed, and I was the Armoured Squadron Commander in the area.

A few months earlier, we had been doing the Junior Command course together at Infantry School in Mhow. Pannu had a Bullet motorcycle. One day Pannu's motorcycle caught fire. and there was one officer from the Armoured Corps whose name was Balbir Sandhu. He was a very good mechanic, and his hobby was repairing automobile engines. He was always offering himself for work, going wherever there was an automobile that was in trouble. He had burnt his hands repairing some instructor's car recently. His hands were swaddled in white bandages. He had freed his fingers to work, and he had shaped his fingernails like a screwdriver. Balbir repaired Pannu's Bullet motorcycle despite burnt hands and bandages. Pannu used to keep his Bullet motorcycle with him wherever he went.

My regiment, Deccan Horse, had come to Pauwwan Da Chak village just short of Chambb. We were the armoured regiment supporting the infantry division deployed there.

For about two months short of the war, I saw him every second or third day. Whenever I had time, I would go over to his company. He was fond of *shikar*, and we used to have lunch together of whatever he had bagged.

He was the Alfa Company Commander of 5 SIKH at Point 303 on the Koel-Moel track, which came to Chambb from Pakistan. That track disappeared into Pakistan across the Line of Control. We spent some very carefree and enjoyable days there before the war.

I had been to his company many times and had spent a lot of time there. I knew the spread of his trenches and emplacements like the back of my hand. I still remember that his protective patrol was located about 600 m ahead on the Koel-Moel track in a derelict village named Dahingawali or some such name.

There were five or six trees there and a dried-up pond towards the left of Point 303. I knew that in case of war, this very ground would be crucial. I used to take my squadron's tank crews at night over this terrain. In the daytime, I would blindfold them and make them walk the folds of the earth to find their bearings. I was just trying to make them absorb the details of topography so thoroughly that they would be able to outfox the enemy when the time came to fight on this very ground.

The men of my squadron, all Sikhs, felt the stress of my training methods. They started complaining that the Squadron Commander was treating them like *bhed-bakri* (sheep and goat), throwing them here and there at odd hours. The griping of the men reached the ears of my Commanding Officer (CO), Lieutenant Colonel JS Bal, a thorough professional and a no-nonsense man. He came to my squadron and told everybody, 'There is going to be a war, and your Squadron Commander is doing the right thing. You have to train hard for it. You will thank him for what he is doing when the time comes. Stop your cribbing. He is training you well. Just follow your Squadron Commander.'

I used to train them in almost everything, and that too at night: escape hatch drills, gunnery emergencies, and so on. As a result, every man of my squadron knew the area between Munnawar and Gurha Ridge like the streets of his own village.

Mine was the first squadron to be inducted into Chambb before the war in November 1971. When the war started, the troops of my squadron were in the areas of Munnawar, Jhanda, Ghuggi, Bania, and Barsala.

When B Squadron was inducted along with the regimental headquarters, I think Major Ginger Bal went on to the Phagla area. I don't know where all he went but I think some of our elements must have been on Mandiala South.

I was at Jhanda. There was a little flow of information coming to us. A lot of troop movements were taking place and lots of actions as well. On 4 December, I was in the 4/1 GR defended area at Jhanda. We were assisting them, firing at the enemy, using our tank machine guns and that sort of thing. The enemy's probing attacks were coming in, which were not like some huge, massed tank attacks coming in. We were busy trying to ward off these small enemy actions.

The enemy's early attacks came in on Munnawar village, which the enemy captured. One of my squadron's officers, Lieutenant SS Gill, was commanding the troop at Munnawar. He had to pull back to Chak Pandit along with the company (or maybe a company less a platoon) located there. After they pulled back, they counterattacked with my tank troop on the morning of 4 December. They regained Munnawar. In retaking it, this brave officer, SS Gill, died. He, too, used to have a red Bullet.

At Jhanda, where I was located, there were no enemy tank attacks. We could see their tanks at a distance, they were supporting their infantry. We were firing on their tanks and their infantry.

One of my troops was in 5 ASSAM with an officer called Varinder. They shot a few tanks – I think two or three – and Varinder got a wound in the eye.

My squadron's second-in-command, Mahender Singh, had a troop with him. When this attack on Munnawar was to take place, I sent him there since I knew that if our men captured Munnawar, they would require additional tanks to strengthen our position. This was now the southern belly of our defences and could easily be turned around by the enemy. But, by that time, Gill had already captured Munnawar.

In the meantime, the regimental headquarters had acted on the Dewa axis. The Adjutant and his troop had shot up some enemy tanks there. The Regimental Headquarters Troop pulled back, and Captain Mahender Singh went to Gurha with his troop. In the fog of war, this information did not reach me.

By now, the enemy was attacking Mandiala North and South. Captain Mahender Singh got injured. He said it was an air strike that got him, and a bullet pierced his nose. He had to be evacuated. Risaldar Bahadur Singh also got something on his back, but the troop remained at Gurha. The enemy got hold of Mandiala North, the highest ridge. It was held by 5 SIKH, and despite counterattacks, Mandiala North couldn't be regained. In the retaking of Mandiala South, Captain Mahender's troop assisted. There were some other actions at Sukhtao Nalla in which my squadron never came into play, but our regiment knocked out many enemy tanks that had been attempting to outflank our positions by infiltrating through the Sukhtao Nalla.

The other action in which I played a part was in the counterattack to recapture Point 303. This was my friend Major Devinder Pannu's company.

On 6 December morning, at about 5 a.m., I got an order from my CO, 'You will have to link up with Point 303.'

I asked him, 'Sir, why link up with Point 303?'

He said, 'Point 303 had fallen to the enemy, but two companies of X battalion have counterattacked, and they have recaptured Point 303. All they now want is tanks to support them against the enemy's next move. The enemy is likely to counterattack to recapture Point 303. You go to Point 303 with your tanks and link up with X battalion there.'

I started with my squadron on the morning of 6 December. I came in via Jhanda and I came to a place, I forget its name, but it is about a kilometre short of Point 303 on the Koel-Moel track.

By now, it was daylight, and enemy aircraft swooped down upon us and started strafing us. We spread out and threw a smoke screen and extricated ourselves from the air attack. The CO sent an additional tank troop led by Captain Kaushik to join us. I had two other troops of my own squadron and my own tank. Luckily, we had lost no tank to the enemy air action. All in all, I had ten T-54 tanks. I also had 39 Medium Regiment's Forward Observation Officer with me. So, I said to him, 'I cannot ask for artillery fire on Point 303 and nor can I fire my own guns on Point 303 as our own infantry could still be there.'

Presupposing this possibility, I thought, 'Let me try to see and confirm what is happening around me.' So, I stood with my squadron about one kilometre short of the objective and tried to catch some sounds. I told my tank driver to shut off the engine. If there were a firefight going on, there would be some sound of bullets being fired and explosions. If our side had already captured Point 303 then the enemy artillery would be shelling Point 303. Nothing of that sort was happening. There was a total inexplainable silence. I didn't like the situation. I got on the radio to my CO and asked him again, 'Are you sure, Sir, that our infantry is there at Point 303?'

He said, 'Yes, yes! You better hurry up and link up with them. They are having a tough time facing the enemy. There is hand-to-hand fighting going on there.'

I was puzzled. Who was feeding all this dramatic commentary to my regimental headquarters and my CO? It was about half past six at that time. I told the CO, 'I don't hear any small arms fire, nor do I hear any artillery shelling noise in the direction of Point 303.'

He said, 'Are you sure you are heading for the right objective?'

I said, 'I know Point 303 very well. It is my friend Major Pannu's company, and all my men also know every inch of the ground here. I have spent days walking all over this area with my complete squadron. It is clear daylight now, not even dark. I can see the Koel-Moel Class 5 track. I can count the trees on Point 303. I recognise the contours of the ridge line. So, I know I am facing the right objective.'

The CO tried to dismiss me, 'It can't be. You are facing some other objective.'

I was taken aback. My CO was doubting me!

I said, 'Sir, please do not doubt me. I know this area like the back of my hand, and I know I am facing Point 303.'

I called all the tanks on the radio who were spread out and hidden and gave my orders, 'That's the objective. You are left of the road incul[1] to you, you are right of the road excul[2] to you. We will not do a conventional attack. Either go line ahead or go extended line. We will go, fire, and move. First bound five hundred metres.

I told Captain Kaushik, 'Kaushik, you will take the first bound and the other two troops (Babu Singh and Lal Singh's troops), who are with me, once they are in position, we advance.'

I was in a quandary. I told them not to fire on the objective unless they attracted tank fire or any other kind of fire.

Kaushik's troop took the first bound. They attracted no enemy fire. Then I started advancing. As soon as we advanced, the air cracked, and we got fired upon. It was broad daylight. Enemy tanks in a hull-down position could easily knock out our tanks advancing in the open towards them. Our only way to get out was to speed up and charge at them, so I gave the order, 'Okay, full speed ahead. The enemy tank fire will be met. No stopping.' Then I sent a report back to the CO on my radio set. 'Sir, contact with enemy established. Enemy tank fire coming on us from the direction of Point 303.'

---

1. inclusive

2. exclusive

Risaldar Babu Singh's troop was on my left. He was a daredevil officer – a Vir Chakra awardee of the 1965 war. His tank was on the extreme left. He saw the hidden enemy tanks firing and their guns flashing. Strictly speaking, you don't break formation in an assault. Risaldar Babu Singh moved off with his tank.

'Where are you moving?' I asked him on the radio set.

He said, 'Wait, Sir. I will go and get that enemy tank that is firing at us. I will join up after getting him.'

He went to the flank and, from an enfiladed position, knocked out the enemy tank that he had seen.

That's the time we observed more enemy tanks on Point 303. There were a couple of enemy tanks, maybe two or three or more, I couldn't say. We didn't open up our guns, we just went full speed ahead. Kaushik's radio cracked, and he said to me, 'Sir, khaki men are in the *sarkanda* all around. Point 303 is full of enemy troops.'

I gave out the order, 'All tanks, use your machine guns; don't fire the main guns.' I feared that while our tanks were charging full speed ahead, we could end up hitting our own tanks due to undulations on the ground.

On the Regimental radio net, the CO, who was listening to my radio transmission, came on the radio frequency and said, 'What is this order of yours?'

I told him, 'Sir, we have already drawn fire. Now you let me deal with the situation myself, and you stay out of it!'

Short of the ridge crest, we slowed down. The khaki infantry had disappeared and melted away. I got out of my tank and crawled to the crest line of the ridge. I saw two Pakistani tanks reversing on the other side of the ridge. I ran back to my tank, and we quickly fired at the enemy tanks. It was their lucky day. They escaped.

It was now around half past seven or maybe eight in the morning of 6 December.

I send a message to my regimental headquarters on the radio set, 'Point 303 taken.'

The CO said on the radio set, 'Sorry! I believe you are on the wrong objective.'

I said, 'Sir, we have had this discussion before. Let me describe the objective as I stand here. This is Major Pannu's company's locality. Seven trees here, there is the dried-up pond here, the Koel-Moel track is running here. There is a *safed butti* (a small memorial/grave) here on the left side. The Phagla Ridge is running to the right. If this place we are at is not Point 303, then I don't know which one is Point 303.'

The CO responded, 'Okay, we will just check.'

By now about half an hour had passed. I sent my tank's radio operator out to scout around and check for our infantry's X battalion, in case they were anywhere close by.

He came back after some time and reported, 'Sir, nobody's around here. No sign of our own infantry. The place is deserted.'

I passed this information to my CO.

Again, he said, 'Let me check.'

At around ten o'clock, on the reverse slope of Phagla Ridge, I watched two companies of the X battalion coming along with their officer. They were being led by a captain or maybe a JCO from 5 SIKH. They had gone and sat on a wrong objective and were cooking up stories and reporting on a radio set of hand-to-hand combat and recapture of Point 303.'

This Sikh leading the column came to my tank and said, 'Sir, they were sitting on the wrong objective. We found them.'

I said to their officer, 'Do you know what you have done? Anyway, this is not the time for recriminations. Go and occupy those trenches. You can expect a counterattack from the enemy.'

I reported this back to my CO.

The story does not end here.

At about 12 o'clock, the squadron of another newly inducted armoured regiment, led by a Major, came to Point 303. They had been sent to relieve me. I was further earmarked to counterattack and recapture Ghogi, Bania, and the Barsala complex – my next task. The enemy had broken through the 5 ASSAM front, and I had to go there to plug the gaps.

Y Armoured Regiment was just reaching Chambb from the rear areas and had just been raised a few months ago in Ahmednagar. They were stepping on the ground in Chambb for the first time. So, I explained the dispositions and the lie of the land to the Major of the Y Armoured Regiment. Then we pulled out of Point 303 and got onto the Koel-Moel track. My CO told me to wait there. Major Ginger Bal, B Squadron, Commander of my regiment, would also be joining me for the planned attack on Ghogi, Bania, and Barsala villages to recapture them.

I met Major Ginger for the first time there since the balloon had gone up, and I said to him, 'Hello Ginger. How's it going?'

He said, 'Great, Sir. I am told we are required to go in for an attack.'

'So it seems. Let's wait for the orders to move into attack. You know the area?'

He said, 'Yes, Sir. I know the area all right.'

Our two squadrons of Deccan Horse were ready to go in for attack – all was set.

But at about two o'clock that night, we received orders from the CO: 'Stand down. No attack to go in.'

Thereafter our regimental headquarters gave us new orders that we had to extricate that night, i.e., the night of 6 December 1971, to the east bank of Munnawar Tawi River and hold the line there. We were to abandon the west bank without fighting.

My friend Major Devinder Pannu had died a soldier's death when the enemy had attacked Point 303. I learnt of the circumstances of the attack on his company in bits and pieces after the war.

On 5 December, the enemy incessantly shelled his company and tried to overrun his position. His company dug in well, and Captain Kamal Bakshi, another officer cast from a steel mould, was his second-in-command. He, too, made the supreme sacrifice in defending Point 303, fighting to the last round.

The enemy had disguised their artillery forward observation officers and infiltrated them into Indian territory just before they attacked, and these enemy artillery observers, with radio sets and maps hiding behind our own positions, were able to direct accurate artillery fire on Point 303 company's defences.

Major Pannu was directing our own artillery fire on the attacking enemy when a large shell splinter tore into his chest. This exploding shell also killed Caesar, Pannu's dog, an English Pointer, who was also with him when he died. He had remained faithfully at his master's feet all throughout the fall of shell and shrapnel. When the stretcher-bearers came for Major Pannu, he said, 'Leave me here only, I can still be of some use to my battalion. I will take an artillery shoot and stall the enemy attack. Get me a working radio set and a map. Mine have been destroyed.'

His troops despaired. The wound was fatal and had nearly cut through half his chest. They lifted their officer and put him on a stretcher. Pannu took out his wallet with a slow movement of his hands and gave it to his batman. 'See to it that my fiancée's photograph is returned to her.' He had recently gotten engaged and was to be married soon.

The stretcher blanket had rubbed against his face and there was sand sticking on his face. Pannu said to his batman, 'Wipe my face clean and brush my moustaches upwards. I would not like to leave this world with my moustaches drooping down.' The soldier wiped clean his officer's face and brushed his fine moustache up.

After some time, Major Pannu passed away with his moustache up, a true leader and a die-hard infantry soldier to his last breath. He deserved the highest decoration.

A new general came in after the war replacing the previous general. He wanted to know how things had happened. A very elaborate sand model exercise was organised so that everyone could describe his actions. I think this was about two months after the war. I was not there for this sand model exercise as my mother had rheumatoid arthritis and had fallen sick, and I had gone on leave to attend to her.

My CO and other officers of my regiment were there attending the Division sand model exercise after the battle. In this recapitulation and discussion, Major N of the Y armoured regiment and this infantry officer of X infantry battalion connived amongst themselves and claimed that they had carried out the counterattack that recaptured Point 303 from the enemy.

Fortunately, the CO of 5 SIKH, who was also present in the exercise, got up and said, 'But wasn't it an officer or junior commissioned officer (JCO) of 5 SIKH who had led these two companies of yours, who were wrongly sitting on Phagla ridge, to the correct location of Point 303? Then how could you have recaptured Point 303?'

That is when the false claims were caught. Had the CO not intervened, my CO would have thought that I had been making up stories and another armoured regiment had done the counterattack on Point 303. Such is the great confusion in actual battle.

My squadron had one officer dead, two officers wounded, two JCOs dead, one wounded, and ten other ranks dead. It was a dear sacrifice. The CO told me that I had been recommended for an MVC. But the citation couldn't go beyond the Division Headquarters. Sam Manekshaw, the Army Chief, had said, 'This division has withdrawn, so no more awards for them.'

I have no regrets, chakra or no chakra. The point is that people should not lie and sugar-coat their achievements; facts must be stated correctly.

In 1975, I did the Staff College course. My instructor was Colonel PK Khanna, MVC, the erstwhile CO of 5 SIKH, during the Battle of Chambb. He said to me, 'Iesh, you have been chosen as a syndicate leader. You were with me in Chambb during the battle there. Would you care to organise a sand model for the entire Staff College as to what happened at Chambb, and the lessons learnt.'

My first question to him was: 'Sir, I don't know about the higher planning of the battle. I was just a Tank Squadron Commander. Do you want me to tell you and all the people about my squadron actions – where all we counterattacked and what all we did?'

He seemed to receive a jolt and said quickly, 'No, no! You go with the official version only, what has been reported in the situation reports by various battalions during the battle. There are too many senior officers here who will become even more powerful in future, and I don't want them to get to know what had really happened in Chambb. Let us go with the official track only. What has happened has happened. No point in raking the fallen leaves now.'

I still have that green scarf of Pannu's turban, and he is still alive in my heart and in my memory.

The Celestial Identity Card

It's a truth universally acknowledged that a soldier who is in possession of an identity card should not lose it, or he would face a sluggish court of inquiry by the dimmest Mr Thompson kind of officer in the formation. It may be half a millennia before the findings are finalised because so many witnesses have to come from the far corners of the Ganga Jamuna tracts and the Brahmaputra way, and they would tell so many convincing and clinching truths that Thompson would find it hard to select the best truth.

However, little known the feelings or views of such a man may be on first entering his battalion, this truth is well fixed on the battalion gate in the form of a salutary message and, thereby, in the mind of every man who has worn the army's pixelated green pants and shirt that the identity card is the property of the government and not someone or the other's daughter or private goat which can be given away.

I had just arrived on posting to a field station, and the officer whom I was relieving said to me with the look of a patient magician trying to pull two rabbits out of his hat instead of one, 'And now, Sir, I have been holding the most important object of our handing taking over to the last.'

I was puzzled, and in my long and rather undistinguished army career, I had never seen a rabbit pulled out of a hat as this officer was now proposing to do in front of my eyes. He selected a key from his silver key chain, and with a flourish, he inserted it and I heard the answering click of the lock. He pulled the drawer and took out a yellow envelope and a typed receipt voucher. He read the voucher with the look of a principal scrutinising the attendance register of his teachers. When he noted that all was well with the voucher, he opened the yellow envelope and pulled out a square transparent plastic sleeve.

'This, Sir, is the identity card of a dead soldier, and please sign here and here.' He said all this while pointing to the space in the voucher sheet where I was required to sign. He was an Ordnance officer who covered every steady advance of his actions with the reinforcement of vouchers and certificates. He believed in the solid protection offered by the walls of signed receipts and vouchers. To him, locks, keys, procedural forms, condemnation boards, issue vouchers, and certified receipt vouchers, indents and demands were all sacred articles, like the *samagree* in the *pooja ki thaali* of the unit pandit ji.

I looked at the small four-square-inch object that he now gave me with the delicacy of an ammunition officer handling the Mark Four detonation fuse.

I saw the face of a young Sikh soldier looking out from the transparent cellophane cover. 'So, this is the dead man's identity card?' I asked.

'Both yes and no, Sir.' He let slip this new information like a magician producing 'water of India' out of an empty jug.

'But you said it's a dead man's identity card!' I exclaimed.

'That is right, Sir, it is the dead man's identity card but the dead man lives,' said the good Ordnance officer with a look of an insurance salesman about to sell a policy to the langar stray dog.

'If he is alive, then give this goddammed identity card to him, why me? What's this Sherlock-Holmes-style mystery "The Adventure of the Dead Man's Identity Card" about?'

Caring for one's identity card is hard enough – tougher than securing the Kohinoor from Shah Shuja, as William Dalrymple has explained in his book *The Return of a King*. And, here I was, being invited to look after another's bloody ID card! The enormity of this new responsibility suddenly hit me with the force of Vulcan's thunderclap. I drank a glass of cool water and hoped it wouldn't give me amoebic dysentery. I needed to breathe fresh air and think things through. Caring for one identity card is hard enough, like caring for some heir to the throne of Ruritania, but caring for another identity card? The idea was preposterous. In my rather long and undistinguished military career that started by doing miles and miles of front rolls in NDA in the previous century till now, when I do miles and miles of expert paper pushing on my desk, I never faced the moral dilemma of looking after two I-cards. I could look after the command of two sections if someone asked me to sign the undertaking in my rather long and undistinguished military career, but looking after two identity cards when I found looking after my own alone such a burden? '*Bhaiya, yeh hum sey naa ho paayee*!'

I needed time to compose myself to shoulder such a heavy responsibility. I needed the ice of cool thought in my head. I needed to meditate on the issue and consult my astrologer and my palmist. They had helped me overcome many grim difficulties in my rather long and undistinguished military career like obtaining casual leave and paternity leave and furlough.

The blue whistling thrush was calling outside. I had seen it dart about in the bushes like a tyre thief prowling in the Thimmaya Enclave car park in Meerut. Wide hills dotted with double-storey houses with painted tin roofs stood on all sides.

The Kashmiri driver who had driven me here had been giving me a running commentary. 'The Line of Control is on that ridge. This area has become prosperous, *gulf se bahoot paisa aata hai idhar*,' he said, pronouncing Gulf as Galaff. An officer had told me the other day, 'Between here and the river, these last 1,000 yards have claimed the lives of 16 officers. Probably, no other stretch of land in the country is redder in the recent history of our country.'

I had gone and read the names carved on our war memorial. Just forlorn names now. Alphabets on stone. I wondered how their families were after they were gone – what their children were doing, how their parents had coped, so many households shattered and damaged forever. A heavy price to pay for the motherland. The fog of anonymity hung over the little square of the war memorial. Sometimes, when a VVIP came, the widows were called in and given a shawl and a blessing as cameras clicked, the Twitter feeds carried the photographs, and the event flowed down on electronic screens and sank away in the Lethe in which soldiers' names go.

The next day, I met the dead man. He was waiting outside my office with the yogic calm look of one who had become resigned to waiting for the train that was running 72 hours late.

He was a pimply-faced young man, and he tied his turban in circular draws around his head. He had been loitering around for many days there, I presumed. I never could find out. He was lean and fair and rather a good-looking youth. Some of the Sikh boys are captivatingly handsome. He had a face with goodness in it, and that made him give out a good aura. He was in his early twenties, and when I called him into my office, he stood like one of those statues of stone on which time glances off.

I started paper pushing and giving off those hundreds of repetitive signatures on registers, forms, letters etc., without which the engine of the Army stalls. Seeing the rapidity with which I scrawled my *dhobi* mark and threw files into the out tray, beating the speed of even Maruti's assembly line, I wanted to paste a notice on my desk: THE BUCK GATHERS SPEED HERE.

The dead man who was alive kept standing patiently. Free of the files and papers after a while, I asked the boy to come and sit across my desk. I grabbed a blank sheet and poised my leaky fountain pen on a white sheet. The quill and ink was ready.

'Speak, O Oracle, start and tell me everything,' I said.

The soldier swallowed air and kept sitting silently. I realised that he must have faced countless hours of interrogation and questioning, and he must have had a tough time, hovering and stuck in the web of uncertainty. His reticence was understandable. I told him I wanted to hear his story to make a story. I was not holding the scales of justice that would tilt fate one way or the other for him or for me; I was just trying to kill blessed Kashmiri time doing my hobby.

There was indecision on his face, and I didn't know whether he would tell me anything, and I didn't even know whether I would write this story. I didn't press him to tell me anything and just left the whole idea behind. I would go round and round, walking on the small 500-metre circuit that our garrison had. And as the route went past troops barracks, I would see the dead man walking – sometimes going to the langar and sometimes going to the water point or going about doing some odd job. At first, I found nothing odd about him, but then, as I saw him a number of times, I felt that he had an odd way of walking for someone so young and in the flush of youthful health.

I noticed other men and the jolly langar dogs, who have more freedom, as the main gate guards let them go out of the iron sheet gates without making any entrees in the gate registers or frisking them. But even more fascinating than the dogs was a bird I found and wrongly thought of as a Himalayan cuckoo till a bird watcher friend corrected me. In Meerut, it was the lineated barbet that serenaded the days with its song, and in Jaipur, the doves cooed incessantly. Here, in these northern mountains, the blue whistling thrush sings but not as sweetly and as tirelessly as the koel of the hot plains of India, which are my home. The koel has more notes and is a songster of the first order and shyer than the blue whistling thrush found in this district. The thrush is a beautiful bird, though, with a dazzling blue coat and a yellow beak. It goes about eating worms and snails, nosing in the flower beds and even between our tin hut barracks. The tin huts become hot in the day, and the post-lunch hours acquire the weight of heat when the duel of digestion starts and the blood courses sluggishly in the veins. Outside in the hills the sun rises every morning, bright and cleansing, and the morning air is strained clean by the power of the night.

The next morning, I saw the sepoy standing outside my office. He had wrapped a black turban in circular bands around his head. '*Saabji*, I will tell you whatever you want to know,' he said.

I hadn't called him, but who was I to refuse to listen to a good story?

'Sir, my name is Jassa Singh.'

'I am aware of your name,' I said, pulling off the lid of my 20-year-old leaky ink pen. I didn't know what had occasioned this change of heart. Probably a *sifarish* (recommendation) for leave if I knew the Army correctly after my rather long and undistinguished military career.

'Sir, two years ago, when I returned from leave, the Coronavirus epidemic was going on. I did quarantine for ten days in the battalion headquarters. Then we had our CO Sahib's interview the next day. As you know, Sahib, as is the practice, in interviews, our personal identity cards hang on the cord around our neck.'

Our talk was taking place in a small tin hut that was my office. A bird was calling on the tree outside, it sounded like the call of the great barbet. As I listened to his words, my eyes couldn't help but stray onto his face, where many pimples had sprouted on his forehead. One doesn't see sepoys whose faces are pock-marked with pimples every day. Jassa Singh could do with some calamine lotion; it was the thing I used in my own years of beauty, but I kept the advice to myself.

'Sir, after the interview I went to the *battalion kote* (armoury) to deposit my identity card as such were the orders. But the Kotiya (Armoury Non-commissioned Officer in-charge) wasn't there, and the battalion kote was locked. So, I went back, assuming that I would be back soon to deposit my identity card in the safe house when the Kotiya again opened the kote. But the same day, I was sent to my company, which was far from the battalion headquarters. So, I put my I-card and my personal kit in my rucksack and went to my company. Then started the usual routine of patrolling in the jungle, *jhaadi*, and *pahaadi* (foot slogging in jungles, bushes, and mountains).'

'How much is the average gear that a soldier carries in such patrolling?' I asked Jassa.

'Sir, with toiletries, mobile phone, charger, power bank, utensils, soap, towel, sleeping bag, ration, food, water bottle, an AK-47, filled magazines, bulletproof vests, helmets, boots, uniform, surveillance equipment, and ground sheet *wagaira, wagaira*, every soldier carryies about 25 kilograms of gear.'

As an officer, it had been years since I had walked up the mountain and down the dale with such crushing weights, but boys like Jassa Singh did it day in and day out. No wonder the army is a young man's arena who has fresh knees and a good spine.

'*Saabji*, this *silsilaa* (routine) of continuous patrolling continued for about two months. The rains started, and we kept going up and down forests and mountains. *Kabhi yahan cordon lagai, kabhi wahan cordon lagai. Kabhi idhar to kabhi udhar. Kabhi geela to kabhi sukha. Kabhi neend milti to kabhi nahi milti. Saraa khel raat kaa hota hai. Night vision lagaa ke baithte raat bhar*. (Sometimes we put a cordon here, sometimes there. Sometimes this way, sometimes that way. Sometimes wet, sometimes dry. Sometimes I got to sleep; sometimes I didn't. The whole game is played at night. We used to sit all night with night vision on.)

'When all this was on, Sir, I forgot totally that I had put my identity card in my backpack's inner zipper pocket. *Kisko yaad rehta hai operations mein? Admi apna khud ke maa-pyu ka naam bhool jaata hai, itna ragda chadhtaa hai shareer ko din raat pahadon me. ID card to door ki baat hai*. (Forgot the I card, the fatigue and discomfort and wear and tear round the clock is so high that one even forgets the name of one's sire and mother, an ID card is a petty trifle to remember in such circumstances when you are out in operations looking for terrorists.)

'One day, we were ordered to move to Ghazala, along a steep ridge that was about 10,000 to 11,000 ft in the Pir Panjals for area domination. That evening, the weather started fogging up, and our patrol found itself in the centre of swirling clouds of fog. The wind had started howling, and soon came the pricks of lashing rain that dug its teeth on our faces. We were to put stops on the slope every 100 m or so. A stop is a group of sepoys deployed to seal the escape of terrorists out of a particular area around which a cordon is put, and we were to put not one cordon but two cordons – an inner cordon and an outer cordon. Darkness came, and the cloud bank obscured the cold kisses of the stars in heaven. The Company Commander Sahib, who was also in the operation with another search party, sent word on the radio that we were to remain alert as terrorists were suspected to be in the area. We had occupied an all-side open *dhok* for the time being since there was only dense fog all around. It was a cold wilderness of occasional rolling meadows that broke into view like spectacular emerald carpets on which the Gujjar Bakarwals lived with their sheep, and the barking of their sheepdogs echoed in the mountains. The forests were mixed on the mountains by steep rock faces that fell off into near vertical cliffs on all sides, and one false step would assure several months in hospital and a few steel implants, if not outright death. We kept sitting and waiting and listening to the sound of the night. The Section Commander tuned into his Motorola and monitored the talk going on between the Company Commander and other parties. Outside, the same fog cloud covered everything, and two or three jawans were looking into NVDs.[1] Then the radio set crackled, and the Company Commander came on the air: "Saab, take the assault party up the slope and look out sharp. There are hostiles here."

'We left our rucksacks in the open dhok and taking all our AKs and ammunition, moved up the slope through the fog. Orders were to stay on and lookout throughout the night.'

What follows is a reconstruction of what possibly transpired later.

Around midnight, three terrorists – Abdul Mujahideen, Mohammad Mujahideen, and Aslam Mujahideen, who had

1. Night Vision Binoculars

slipped through the Army dragnet, came to the Gujjar Bakarwal dhok, planning to spend the night there.

'*Alhamdulillah*, we arrive safely; by Allah's grace, we will get a few hours of peaceful sleep. Aslam, you be the first one to give watch. Muhammad, you will relieve him at 2 a.m.'

'Ya Allah! What is this, Ustaad? Looks like there have been visitors here. What shall we do?' said terrorist Aslam, as his eyes scanned the neat row of olive green rucksacks of the soldiers in the dhok.

'The kaffir fauj has been here. If they have left their packs here, they must be close by. Let us hide here and kill them all when they come back,' said Muhammad terrorist.

'*Oye, terey ko shaheed hone ka bada shauk hai* (You seem eager to quit this world). Aren't you getting enough *hoors* every now and then here that you want the 72 in heaven? *Faujiyon ko maarna itna asaan hota to Kashmir kabka azaad ho chuka hotan* (If it was so easy to wipe out these RR soldiers, then Kashmir would have become independent 30 years ago). We are not here to get killed, understood?' said Abdul Mujahideen, who was clearly the leader of the pack.

'*To kyaa karen murshid*?' asked Muhammad Mujahideen, who belonged to Abbottabad in Pakistan and had come on a two-year contract posting to Indian Kashmir. Now he had become so fond of the apple-cheeked and doe-eyed beauties of Kashmir that he had requested his handlers that he was willing to do an extended stint of another two years on extremely compassionate grounds with CI ops allowance thrown in, and he sent a DO letter to ISI headquarters MS Branch to kindly extend his foreign posting tenure.

'Idiot! Don't stand there like a handpump. Count how many packs are there,' Abdul snapped at Aslam.

'Sir, there must be ten faujis as there are ten packs.'

'*Achha, aisa karo*, search all the packs. *Inshallah koi khazana mill jaaye* (Lord willing, we may find something useful).'

Muhammad and Aslam took out miniature LED lights and started rummaging through the soldiers' rucksacks, laying out the contents on a ground sheet.

'Found anything useful?' snapped Abdul who wanted to be done with the job and get going as he could smell the ominous presence of jawans very close by. Actually, it was the packs and blankets and sleeping bags that were smelling. The RR soldiers carry their world on their backs as they do not know on which new mountain they will see the next sunset.

Up on the slope, not 50 yards away, Jassa Singh suddenly woke up as his head struck the ground. He hadn't realised but he had fallen asleep sitting. The soldiers have to sit for hours without making noise.

The JCO cursed angrily when he heard the AK and magazines make noise. 'Shhshhh! We are sitting in an ambush, boys. No sounds please,' he whispered. Jassa Singh pinched himself hard, took out some red chilli powder mixed with salt and locked it. The red pepper burned his tongue and the pain for the time being kept sleep at bay.

Down the slope in the fog-obliterated night, in the open dhok, Abdul was systematically going over everything that the soldiers' rucksacks contained. Muhammad was chewing stale *aloo poori*[2] that he had found in a jawan's pack and Aslam was tasting a *shakkar parra*[3] that they had found in the rucksacks of the jawans.

'*Alhamdullilah bhai jaan. Aap bhi khaa len.* The aloo poori is really tasty. *Inshallah agla khana pata nahi kab naseeb hoga.* (Who knows when we will be able to get the next meal.)' He

2. Potato curry with Indian fried bread

3. A sweet confectionary item

munched roughly and quickly like a rhesus monkey does. Abdul was older to them by half a dozen years but a six-year gap in the life of a terrorist made him into a veteran Tarzan.

'*Tum yahan aloo poori khao, khabees gadho. Fauj aa gayi to teeno maarey jaayengey.* (While you two eat aloo poori if the army comes, that would be the end of all three of us.)'

Aslam started collecting Milkmaid tins that he had found and a small Primus stove in his rucksack. '*Waah*! What a neat stove. Now we will not go without tea, *bhaijaan*,' said Aslam as he indulged in the welcome act of scrounging things from the rucksacks.

'Abdul *bhai, aap khaa len. Kam se kam Allah ke ghar bhooke to nahin pahunchengey.* (You also eat, Abdul brother, lest we enter the door of heaven on an empty belly.)'

'Aslam and Mohammad, have you emptied all the fauji rucksacks, found anything more useful than filling your bellies like thieves?' Abdul whispered menacingly.

Nothing else here, bhaijaan. Only battery chargers, leads, and power packs. We have taken the best. The phones the sepoys have taken with them, wherever they have gone. It is strange that they didn't leave a guard party to guard their stuff. How did the Army come to know that we are in this area?' said Mohammad.

'Both of you, make a pile of all their rucksacks and sheets and stuff,' ordered Abdul. The other two terrorists started collecting the backpacks and Aslam opened the inner zip pocket of every backpack. The light from the tiny LED light with which he was working in the dark fell upon the object that his fingers had found—some paper and a square object. Many of the backpacks had yielded bank notes, but he had caught a better fish this time.

Aslam took the object to Abdul. 'Do I throw this also in the pyre to burn, bhaijaan?'

'Show me what you found first,' said Abdul. He threw the light on the hard plastic cover, and the face of Sepoy Jassa Singh, bearded and in a turban, looked back at Abdul.

'Well done, boy. This is good. *Ye kaam ki cheez hai. Isse sambhaal ke rakho.* (This is a valuable thing. Keep it safely.)'

The plumes of fog blew about in the dhok, and the three Mujahideens lit the fire with a ten-rupee Chinese cigarette lighter. They stood there as the fire increased, and the olive-green nylon combat backpacks caught fire. Abdul picked up a stick and turned the articles in the fire so that everything in the pile finally started burning and it would now be impossible to stop the fire. The three terrorists went out of the dhok and heard the crackle and spit of fire after they had warmed their hands over it for a few minutes. Then, suddenly, one of the battery power packs of a mobile phone exploded like a hand grenade going off. The explosion threw slivers of burning nylon all around.

Up on the slope, the sepoys sitting in ambush also heard the explosion. 'What the hell was that? The sound came from down the slope.' The combat team reported the sound to other teams in the area. None of the teams had fired anything.

'Go down to the dhok and have a look,' ordered the team leader. Jassa Singh and a few other sepoys inched down the slope in the pitch darkness slowly, like a snail feeling its way. It took them a long time to creep down the few dozen yards of the slope, and then they saw the yellow tongues of flame spilling out of the dhok and fading out in the dark fog. The fog was glowing yellow like a lampshade, and around it was the black night.

Inexperienced soldiers would have straight away rushed in; slaves to the first impulse. But these men had learnt that in this game you had to out-think the enemy to live to fight another day. The fire could be a perfect bait to lure them into an ambush, thought Jassa Singh, for who except terrorists would burn down the gear and bivouac of jawans.

'Don't go near it. It could be booby-trapped or it can be an ambush. We will wait till morning,' came the Subedar's voice on the Motorola radio set.

In the morning, the sepoys crawled down to the dhok. All their rucksacks had been burnt. Black ashes lay about the mud floor. Jassa realised that his identity card, which was in his rucksack, had burnt, too.

Later, when Jassa informed his officer that his identity card was in his ruck sack that got burnt, the officer suspected Jassa of lying. The officer was convinced that Jassa had lost his identity card while on leave and was trying to cover up his offence. A cloud of suspicion hung above Jassa Singh's name. A court of inquiry was ordered, and he was found guilty of losing his identity card due to personal neglect and was punished.

About a month later, enemy videos started circulating on various enemy-operated social media handles that terrorists had killed many *kaffir* Indian soldiers, and they showed Jassa Singh's Identity Card in their fake video reels as proof of them causing casualties of Indian soldiers.

Singh's innocence was proven, but the identity card was still with the terrorists, and he had been declared dead by them. As fate willed, in a subsequent skirmish with the Army, one of the terrorists escaped the dragnet but left his backpack behind. When the Army examined its contents, one of the things found was Jassa Singh's Identity Card.

It was time to make him officially alive again.

Till My Eyes Can See

The only stories of valour to be believed are those that are told by your enemies about you. Military fighting units always exaggerate and spin stories of their successes and blackout failures from the reports and records. It is the normal tendency of armies of the Indian subcontinent. Many a time, disproportionate honours are accorded to average incidental actions out of political necessity or zeal of particular commanders to feather their own careers by projecting the units under their command as having performed superhumanly. This tendency to bounce staid mediocrity and incidental opportunism to heroism by the strokes of untruthful pens is very common. As a result, we cannot make out wheat from chaff. We do not know our real heroes apart from those created in the fog of war by slick and good use of opportunity and quick and imaginative words and fiction writing in citations. You can write hundreds of enemies killed or squadrons of enemy tanks knocked out, but who is going to go on the ground to verify?

My interest in pursuing this story arose after reading an article by a Pakistani military historian, Major Agha Humayun Amin, on the open source media, who is known for his blunt honesty. In the article, he wrote:

When I joined my tank regiment, 11 Cavalry, on 27 March 1983, I was sent to sub-calibre ranges, which were to become a central part of my life throughout my military career. Somehow, I was either sent to sub-calibre ranges, whether it was 58 Cavalry or 15th Lancers[1] or I decided to go to sub-calibre ranges when I was in command of 5 Independent Armoured Squadron. This place enriched my knowledge of military history. Here, I met tank crews of the 11th Cavalry—a tank regiment that had spearheaded the attack on India in the Chhamb sector on 4 December 1971.

Here at the ranges, the tank crews of the 11 Cavalry always discussed one particular battle, and that was the Battle of Mandiala on 4th December 1971. Mandiala is a ridge north of Chhamb village. Daffadar Bashir was in that battle that day. He belonged to Pind Dadan Khan and was my very dear friend in 11 Cavalry, and later, he was reallotted to 58 Cavalry. His tank was hit by Indian tank fire, but being the driver of his tank, he survived as tank T-59's drivers, being least exposed, always do.

Daffadar Bashir was my troop daffadar in a newly raised regiment of tanks to which he was shifted. He narrated to me the trauma and shock of the battle.

Every Pakistani military historian whom I read who has written about this battle has whitewashed or blacked out the net psychological impact of this battle on the Pakistan Army,

1. Names of Pakistan Army's tank regiment

whether it was the lowest level tank crew of 11 Cavalry or the highest level of Pakistani operational command i.e., 23 Division Headquarters, including the general commanding the division, Major General Iftikhar Khan Janjua. The intricate problem in writing military history or any type of history is that the events and feelings of direct participants can be changed by the writer.

As per 11 Cavalry's direct participants, the tank crews who were there on that day, whom I interviewed from 1983 till date, the Mandiala battle shook 11 Cavalry from top to bottom, and the atmosphere that evening of 4th December was most demoralising and gloomy. 11 tanks were destroyed by Indian tank fire—a complete squadron written off in a few hours on the first day. Perception and decision-making powers of the 23 Division were severely shaken, damaged and malfunctioning. This point is hoodwinked by all Pakistani military historians whom I have so far read. That Alfa Squadron of tanks was lost on 4th December 1971 was a well-known fact when I joined 11 Cavalry in March 1983.

I was rather surprised and deeply impressed by such a candid admission of one's own casualties and failure in a military article. Who were the Indian elements responsible for wreaking such devastation upon 11 Cavalry tanks in the battle of Mandiala? Do we recognise them in our own military history, or have they gone unrecorded for the pen of Herodotus so far?

I was sitting in the army club with some officers of the armoured corps drinking scotch, and like all armoured corps officers, they were fond of talking and chit-chatting. I asked them, 'Sir, does the Armoured Corps of India have any recognised ace tank gunner in its history?'

Colonel X, a very warm and social mud co-officer who has about thirty years of service, took a contemplative sip of whisky soda and said, '*Bhai, hamne to* CQMH *Abdul Hamid ka hi naam suna hai, usne dushman ke teen tank udaayey they, baaki PVC to jyaada tarr leadership roles ke liyey he milley hain* (Brother, we have only heard of CQMH Abdul Hamid who destroyed 3 enemy tanks in the war of 71, other PVCs have usually been granted for leadership roles.)'

Since I was researching tank battles because I would be writing about them, I wanted to do my homework properly. An honest piece of writing should come from empathy and understanding. I spent a couple of thousand rupees on Amazon to purchase the classic books on tank warfare like *Alamein to Zem Zem* by Keith Douglas, *Brazen Chariots, and The Gods Were Neutral* by Bob Crisp, and *Take These Men* by Cyril Joly. These books left an everlasting impression of how it would have been inside the tanks, in the fug of four smelly bodies living inside a noisy and dark iron machine that either kills others or gets killed and from which what is left of the human body is scraped out with spoons. The human tissues of men trained into the machine, in a split second changed physical form and became black and red glue paste like Fevicol when the tank brewed up, and spread on every knob and iron part like a boiling rain. But before the horrors of war, every story starts somewhere:

~

The tanks were lined up in a sandy riverbed facing a hillside. It was the month of May, and the hot wind that continued from sunup till midnight was already remorselessly blowing, heating up everything. There was a lull in the field firing of the main guns of the tanks. Some sowars brought a field table and field chairs and laid it out on a tank. The tank was a Russian T-54, and it had the Broad Arrow number UX 889. The commanding officer and a squadron commander climbed on the tank and started having lunch. They were discussing the performance of the tank crews at the firing range. The regiment was at Ambala, and they were camped in Narayangarh Ranges. The officers finished their lunch, and the Regiment's food lorry drove away. The squadron commander, a tall, wiry, serious professional officer, had been hearing noises coming from inside the tank. He got up and lifted the cupola hatch. There was a sowar inside the tank.

'What are you doing inside?' the officer asked.

'Sahib, I am cleaning the rounds and filling them in the bins for firing,' replied the sowar.

'Have you had your food?' the officer asked.

'No sir.'

'The food lorry has left and there is no food now.'

'*Koi baat nahi sahib, roti me shaam ko khaa loonga, mera kaam zaroori hai.*(Sir, I will eat in the evening, my duty takes priority over eating food.)'

'Who is the chap inside?' asks the commanding officer.

'Sir, it's Sowar Jai Singh of Bravo Squadron. He has missed lunch and is cleaning the ammunition inside his tank,' replied the squadron commander.

'I was looking at the result sheet. Isn't he the same boy whose shooting is very good?'

'Yes sir.'

'Send him to Nagar for Grade One gunner course.'

'Right, sir.'

The squadron commander leaned over the cupola and said, 'Jai Singh, you come with me in the evening when I go back.'

That evening, I came back with Captain Rikhye Sahib. He was the Alfa Squadron commander, but since the Bravo Squadron commander was away on some leave or course or temporary duty, Rikhye Sahib was, for the time being, in-charge of the Bravo Squadron also. The next day, Sahib called me to his office and told me, 'You will go for the Grade One Gunner course to Ahmednagar. Pack your bags and do well.'

I was very hesitant. I said to my officer, 'Sahib, *merey se senior bahut log hain.* (Sir, there are so many people who are senior to me who are still Grade 2 gunners. They will eat me alive if you send me for Grade 1 before them.)'

Sahib said, '*Agar seniority se Grade One Gunner bantey to apni adhi se jyaada regiment ke gunners grade 1 hotey.* (If it was possible to make grade one gunners based on the length of service, then more than half the Regiment's tank gunners would already be Grade 1 gunners. you see. I will ensure that nobody says anything to you. You prepare to go for the course and do well on the course.)'

So, I left for Ahmednagar.

When I reported with my documents, the clerk said, 'You go back to your regiment, you can't do this course.'

I asked him, why couldn't I do the Grade One gunner course.

'Because you have not yet completed 5 years of service, which is the minimum required to be eligible for this course. Did nobody tell this to you in your regiment before they sent you here? *Yu he mooh utha ke chaley aatey ho.*'

I was worried about what should I do next. How could I go back to my regiment when my squadron commander sahib had ordered me for this course? That afternoon, I was standing in line in the *langar* to take food when I heard two men ahead of me talking to each other. I didn't know these men, but they were talking about the officer in charge of training. By their talk I could make out that he was from my part of the country. The next morning, I went to the training officer's office and saluted him. I told him my problem about how I was being returned to my unit without doing the course due to some stupid regulation which made no sense. The officer said, 'You will be on the list. Don't worry. You will do the course and do it well.'

That's how I did my Gunnery Grade One course. When I returned from the course, my regiment had moved to PDC—Pauwwan Da Chak village near Chhamb from Ambala. I went to PDC, and since I had been judged the best gunner in the course, in the next Commanding Officers durbar, my CO sahib gave a prize in front of the whole regiment that I had earned *izzat* for my regiment.

Though I was from Bravo Squadron, which was the Jat Squadron, I was now allotted to the Regimental Headquarter Troop (RHQ Troop), since the RHQ Troop had the Regiment's best gunners. I came to UX 889 which was the Adjutant Sahib's tank.

One day, the prime minister, Indira Gandhi, the army chief Sam Maneckshaw, and Babu Jagjiwan Ram came for our entire division's durbar. I still remember Babu Jagjiwan Ram's words that he had spoken while addressing us:

'The best weapon is no good if the hands using them are weak and incompetent and if the heart is weak. No weapon can compensate for the man. It's just a thing made of iron parts.'

Many years after the 1971 War, there was a competition of armoured units in Jaipur. The 2nd Lancers regiment organised the event. A .22 rifle bracket was mounted on the tank's main gun, which had to be rotated manually to align with various targets. In thirty seconds, one had to fire four times on four different targets.

I hit all 4 targets in 26 seconds and the person who was coming second missed all four targets. The officers of his regiment said, 'Jai Singh has scored by a lucky fluke. He can't be that good.'

I said to the officers, 'Please let's have it again. If I miss even one target out of four, I will take off my uniform right here, leave the army forever, and go back to my village.'

They did two more trials. I hit all four targets every time in 23 and 24 seconds. Then, the same officers who said I had scored by fluke even came to see me off at Jaipur Railway Station when I was going back to my regiment after winning the competition.

On the third of December 1971, at about 5 p.m., we received orders to start moving to our battle-ready positions. My tank commander was Captain Surender Kaushik Sahib, who was from Jaipur. Around 8 pm, Pakistani artillery started shelling our positions. The entire route was jam-packed with villagers fleeing with their possessions and animals. We made our way slowly forward towards Gurha high ground which overlooked the wide Sukh Tao Nallah. Here, we deployed in a wide semi-circle along with Major Ginger Bal Sahib's Bravo Squadron (Jat Squadron).

We took our UX 889 into an RCL gun pit already dug by the troops of 5 Sikh regiment. We needed to widen it to accommodate a tank. So, we got on the task with *kassis* and widened it enough for our tank. It was a moonlit night. Kaushik sahib said, 'Go in front and see if the tank is visible from the enemy side.'

We camouflaged our tank, and there was natural undergrowth of bushes that gave it good cover. It was a moonlit night, and we hid our tank in such a manner that even we couldn't detect it from one hundred yards distance. We had about hundred and fifty litres drinking water, roasted gram (*bhoogdey*) and *shakarparas* to live on. Ours was a command tank with two radio sets for adjutant sahib to communicate with regimental headquarters. We were wearing black battle dress with rubber-soled DMS boots, and our tank had 44 rounds—a mix of heavy Armour Piercing Discarding Sabot (APDS) rounds, High Explosive Anti-Tank (HEAT) rounds, and High Explosive (HE) rounds. The first two types of rounds were to destroy enemy tanks. HE rounds could be used on enemy infantry concentrations and soft-skinned vehicles.

It was cold, and we settled down in our *marundis* (warm coats), talking among ourselves. We had no idea what would happen next. The enemy artillery shelling had ceased, and inside our tank, we could only hear loudly each other's chest heaving and breathing. Kaushik Sahib was listening on the radio set.

At about half past six, the sky started turning grey and the night went away. I rubbed my eyes and sprinkled some water into my eyes. Captain Sahib was standing out of the cupola with only his head out and looking through his binoculars. I could imagine that all our tank commanders must have been doing the same thing till the two kilometres extended semi-circles where they were all in hull-down positions covering the wide Sukh Tao Nallah. We had nodded off to sleep in awkward stances. The driver's face was resting on the dials, and my head was on the breech block of the main gun. Everyone was awake now, expectation and uncertainty pressurised our eyes, and our ears felt warm.

Captain Sahab spoke, 'Enemy tank column approaching 10 o'clock, range about 2000 metres.'

I focused on the gun sight and rotated the turret in the direction that Captain Sahib had indicated.

'Ji sahib, I can see them but only dimly.'

It was still dark outside as the day was just breaking. We had to allow them to come closer. The Paki tanks had crossed the border in the night and crept into India through the Sukhtao Tau Nallah. A wide seasonal water channel with many dry channels and clumps of *sarkanda* grass. It flowed in from the Pakistani side of the border into our territory to empty into the Tawi River. The Paki T-59s had crept into India at a very slow speed in the night.

'Jai Singh, wait now, let them come closer. The light will also increase with each passing minute.'

Captain Sahib had alerted the rest of the squadron on the radio net. It seemed that a complete armoured regiment was headed our way through the Nallah. When I looked through my sights, I saw that the Pakistani tank crews were riding on their tanks like people sitting on a camel or an elephant going to a *mela* (country fair).

'Sahib, the way they are sitting on their turrets, it looks like they are going to a mela.'

Three Paki tanks were moving ahead and came into my range. I fired at the third tank. It brewed up immediately when the APDS round hit it. It burst up in flames in a second. The lead tank kept on moving ahead without realising that I had hit a tank behind him.

I had been aiming at the white band that the Pakistani tanks had on their turrets. It was like a hangman's noose that they had placed on the turrets of their tanks. What could be more thoughtful and helpful for an enemy gunner than a bright one-foot wide *patti* (strip) that the enemy had painted in a circle running all around the turret of their tanks? Then I turned my main gun on the leading tank whose crew had no idea that it was being stalked by my gun sight. I again aimed at the white band and the APDS round penetrated and the T-59 brewed up.

The crew of the second tank which was in the middle, saw the other two tanks burning and jumped from their tank and started running away, as if forewarned about what was going to happen to it. I aimed and fired at the tank. It went up in flames. There were four RCL jeeps that were following the tanks. They also met a similar fate at my hands. By now, having realised the presence of Indian tanks on Gura, the enemy tanks started jockeying and hiding behind clumps of sarkanda grass and mounds and folds in the Sukh Tau Nallah.

As the day progressed, many of our commanders like Jindiya Maharaja Jasbir Singh Sahib, Mathur Sahab, 5 Sikh CO sahib *wagaira wagaira* (etc., etc.) also came to watch the scene from Mandiala top.

As the day progressed, I got three more enemy tanks with my first shot. Towards late evening that day, around 5 p.m., I spotted an enemy tank at the extreme range of my main gun. It was dodging and running away.

Captain sahib said, 'Jai Singh, *ye bhaag nikla, ye bachh gyaa.* (He has run away; he will get saved.)'

'Sahib, *jabb tak ye meri aankhon ko dikh rha hai,ye bacheyga nhi.* (Sir till my eyes can see him, he will not get away.)'

That T-59 kept dodging me, it took cover in a mango orchard. I had fired four rounds at him and missed him. He was over three kilometres away. I was furious with myself. I never missed a tank with my first round. This clever adversary had evaded me four times. I must use a ruse. I laid my gun in a gap of which I knew. He would have to turn his tank there, and I waited for him. My estimate was right. He was creeping into the gap, my gun was already laid, and I pressed the fire button. The round went like an arrow and hit the tank. It was almost dark now, and my eyepiece was filled with blazing showers of orange flame.

Darkness came like a friend for enemy tanks. I knew they would withdraw safely now and get into a league. I had only two rounds left in my tank by the end of the day. We sent out the radio message, 'Get me *chappati* for *haathi*.' We filled up our tank with ammunition and waited in the night. At about 4 a.m., I was feeling uneasy and wanted to go out of the tank to freshen up. I slipped out of the hatch plate on the floor of the tank. I had gone about fifty yards and was searching for a bush to sit behind when I saw the shapes of two tanks. Could these be our own tanks? I walked closer and saw that the tanks had white paint bands on their turrets. I forgot all about my morning job and ran back to my tent, slid under it and got in. I told Captain Sahib, 'Sahib, two enemy tanks are very close to us.'

Captain Sahib opened the cupola, verified it, and said to me, 'Get them.'

I hit the first tank straight away. The second tank started its engine, and its exhaust pipe threw out helpful sparks that helped me identify its position. We hit the second tank also. It was not even 24 hours since I had fired my first round, but I had knocked out nine enemy tanks already.

On 4th December, we received orders to go for a counterattack on the only bridge that had fallen to the enemy. We gave overhead fire, and a platoon of 5 Sikh, led by a very brave JCO, cleared the bridge. Some of his jawans were reluctant to follow him. He had shouted in Punjabi at them. I had heard him shout, 'Have you joined the army to chicken out? What are you afraid of? I will be right in front of all of you. I will be the first one to catch a bullet. *Karwai* (Action) will be continued till the bridge is secured.'

The bridge was cleared of the enemy, and by 5 p.m., we drove back to our position at Gura.

On 5th, we received orders to Attack Point 303. We drove in extended line in third gear. We crossed enemy tanks; they were going fast in opposite direction from ours, but we couldn't stop. Our orders were to make it to Point 303. The sarkanda was full of enemy infantry. We were crossing a pond and there were two enemy tanks on the other side of it. I shot these three tanks, and we reached Point 303. I even saw Major Pannu's, the infantry company commander's, dead body. I saw many things happening, but it would be better not to mention them.

On 8th December, a troop of three enemy tanks of 28 cavalry, I think, waded through the Tawi and emerged on our bank. These were also T-59s and I engaged and destroyed them at 9 a.m.

After 8th December, our tank was sent as a protection tank for the divisional operational room or tactical headquarters.

Thus ends the wartime story of Jai Singh Sahib of Deccan Horse, probably the only ace tank gunner of the Indian Army with a score of 15 tanks to his name in the Battle of Chhamb in the 1971 Indo-Pak War. No enemy tank, which had the misfortune to come into the vision of his gun sight, escaped destruction. Till his eyes could see, he got them.

Major Dhyan Chand's Tooth

The Indian Hockey team returned after winning a glorious medal for India in the Paris Olympics 2024. The Indian hockey team's captain, Harmanpreet Singh, visited the Golden Temple, and after that, he went to garland the statue of Major Dhyan Chand outside the stadium in Delhi. Judge for yourself why Major Dhyan Chand is so much loved by hockey players after reading this true story of events in the Berlin Olympics in 1936, Nazi Germany.

In Jhansi, his home town, he was affectionately called Dadda (elder brother). He was a little bronze-coloured old man who used to walk slowly with a forward stoop.

'Dadda, why do you bend in front when you walk?' we kids would ask him. We all knew he was the great Dhyan Chand, the hockey wizard of India.

'*Saaree umar hockey ball dribble kee hai* (I have spent my life dribbling a hockey stick),' he would say with a smile. '*Abb peeth seedhee nahi hoti* (Now my back doesn't straighten up even if I want).'

'Dadda, tell us what happened at the Berlin Olympic games?' I wanted to hear the famous incident from his own mouth.

'*Haan, kyuu nahi*. (Yes, why not.) *Dekho bhai, aisa thaa ki* (Look, it was like this) that Hitler was not a sports fan or something. He was not in favour of hosting the 1936 Olympic games in Germany. Berlin had been nominated as the venue for the next Olympic games before the Nazi Party came to power. Germany was in the middle of a massive secret rearmament programme in 1936. Hitler had his hands full of imperial dreams for Germany, but then he thought of showing the world how great his Aryan German race was through the Olympics.'

It felt wonderful to hear of the events from the mouth of a man who had been there, whose eyes had seen the very personalities, and who had been in the scheme of great things.

Dadda continued, 'It was Goebbels who was the propaganda minister of the Third Reich. He persuaded Hitler. He said, "My Führer, look what glory it shall bring the fatherland. Our Aryan athletes will wrap up all the top spots and win everything. Can there be greater glory for Germany under the Swastika? The world shall know of the racial supremacy of the Aryan master race. All races will be shown as inferior to ours. It is also a great opportunity to showcase our efficiency as a nation to the world. There can't be a better way to show the world our resurgent nation." So, the Nazis went ahead with the games with a political aim.

'In the opening ceremony on the first of August, we Indians were dressed in white coat pants, and we had sky blue turbans with golden *kullaas* on our heads. Every contingent was told to do the raised-arm Olympic salute that was like the Nazi salute when it passed the grand podium where the German dictator Hitler and his Reichsmarschall were sitting. We had decided that we would not give Hitler the Nazi salute as we passed the grandstand.

'*Beta*, when we marched, we raised our hands to our forehead and did *salaam*, Indian style, to the German grandstand, which was full of grey-coloured German uniforms. Hitler, with his distinctive toothbrush moustaches, sat next to a very fat German, his number two in the Nazi hierarchy. The fat German was Goring, who was in charge of their air force also. When the crowd saw the Indians not salute their leader, they started booing. The stadium was huge and jam-packed. The Nazis had managed everything very efficiently and in their grand theatrical manner with hundreds of German Eagles on tall poles and the red flag with a crooked cross in a white circle fluttering against the blue sky on the rim of the Olympic stadium. Whenever Hitler stood and returned a salute, the stadium erupted in loud shouts of *Seig Heil, Seig Heil.*

'You see, we were part of British-administered India and, for the time being, a part of the British Empire. The Germans only had contempt for us beneath their polite exteriors.'

'Dadda, what happened after this? Were Indians mistreated?'

'Not at all. The Germans were at their best behaviour all the time with us. They wanted to have a warm-up match with us, a friendly match on the first or second day. So eager were they to size us up and, if possible, to trample us into the dust on the hockey field. So, we had a practise match with them in which they defeated our team soundly by four goals to one. This news spread very quickly that the Germans had defeated India, the previous two-time Olympic champions, in hockey.

'One of our forwards was out of form and not playing at his optimum. An urgent telegram was sent to India asking for Captain Ali Iqtedar Shah, also of the Punjab Regiment, like me. A very fine hockey player. He was called Dara by us, his teammates, and had been refused leave by his battalion's *angrez* commanding officer to participate in the Olympics. The defeat at the hands of the new and formidable German team had made every one of us nervous, and for a time after the practice match, we felt unsure of ourselves. Dara was airlifted from India and flown to Germany and managed to reach us just before the semi-finals with France. We managed to scrape through to the finals with Germany, with Dara joining the team in the nick of time.

'And whom do we meet in the finals? The Germans, who had played in top form all throughout. That day was 15 August 1936, later to be our Independence Day. The stadium was filled to full capacity. All of Berlin seemed to have come to watch the match. Hitler himself came to see this match. He had been told by his flatterers that the German team would make mincemeat of the Indians and get sweet revenge for showing disrespect to their Führer and Germany during the opening ceremony.

'The final hockey match began, and try however much, we were thwarted by a solid, impenetrable wall of German defence and no ball would go into the German goal. The crowd sat on the edge of their seats and cheered the Germans each time they came towards the Indian goal only to return without scoring. Anyhow, we kept trying and scored one goal only. When the halftime came, we were leading by just one goal, and the Germans hadn't yet opened their account. But they seemed very confident now.'

'Dadda, what do you feel was the reason that you were unable to score goals quickly?' I asked in my eagerness all of a sudden, unable to hold my suspense.

'Mujhey lagaa ki wo German goal size me thoda chotaa tha (I felt that the opponent's goal mouth was smaller). I had that sense throughout the first half, but anyhow, the halftime came, and we had scored once. If we held on to our lead, we would win the match. I decided to change into my ordinary rubber-soled army PT shoes (cheap ordinary canvas shoes with rubber soles) and took off the more modern spiked shoes and stockings. The teams

changed sides at halftime, and we now had to shoot at our own goalpost that we had been defending in the first half of the match. This goal had the standard-sized goal mouth. Soon we scored five goals in the second half. We were on a roll. I again went piercing through the German defence to score a goal and their goalkeeper deliberately whacked my face with his hockey while trying to save a goal. Blood ran from my mouth, and I was taken for first aid and came back after dressing. I called my teammates and told them, "They are stooping to unsportsmanlike play now in frustration. We need to teach them a lesson in Indian ball control and show what Indian hockey is all about."

'We decided that we would not let the Germans touch the ball, try however much they would for the remainder of the match. We would keep possession of the ball. For the rest of the match, we kept them running like monkeys all over the field. We kept passing the ball forward and backwards by long passes, and the Germans kept sprinting all over the length of the field to get the ball.

'Hitler left the match soon because he did not want to present the gold medal to the Indian side. He was a race-prejudiced dictator. We made the Germans dance in circles in front of their home crowd and won the match by eight goals to one. The crowd groaned loudly.

'In anticipation of their grand hockey victory, the Germans had kept a celebration dinner and had already sent us an invitation. It was meant only for the two finalist teams. They had already thought that we would be runners-up to Germany.

'At the dinner party, many senior Nazis came. A German captain, aide de camp to Hitler, came to me and said in English, "*Herr Hockey Kapitan*, are you Dhyan Chand of the Indian side? The Führer desires to meet you."

'I understood him. Most of us could speak passable English, but I said in Hindi, "*Chalo*. (Let's go.)"

'I followed him to the group of cross-bejeweled officers. The Germans loved wearing lots of decoration crosses on their uniforms. Like the maths symbol of addition, it looked. Hitler stood talking to a group of senior Nazis like Goring, Hess, Speer, Goebells. *wagairah, wagairah.*

'"*Mein* Führer, the Indian team Captain," announced his ADC.

'Hitler looked at me from top to bottom. I did a salaam. I was wearing my official white coat and pant, and my canvas PT shoes, the only pair of shoes I had carried with me. I must have looked rather under-attired for this grand dinner party to Hitler.

'"You played very well, like a wizard, and I am told you had an injury also. How is it now?" enquired Hitler politely. His translator translated.

'Thank you, Sir. I only left one tooth in Germany in today's match, but otherwise, I am fine. The German team played very well, and your hospitality has been very good. We are all well looked after.

'The German translated my answer to Hitler. The gathering was amused, and Hitler started laughing at my joke about leaving a tooth behind on German soil.

'"What is your share in the world's work when not playing hockey?" asked the dictator showing amusement and further interest.

'*Janaab*, I am in the Indian Army,' I replied.

'"Is it? And what is your rank?" enquired Hitler.

'Janaab, I am a Naik in the Punjab Regiment.' I said.

'"What is Punjab Regiment?" he wanted to understand.

'Janab, it is an infantry regiment.

'When my answer was translated to Hitler, his eyes widened in astonishment and warmth shined in his manner. He said, "I was also in the infantry in the previous great war." Then he continued, "A Corporal, that's all. A man of your ability, prowess, and will, and only a corporal. The British don't value your worth. Come to Germany, and I will make you an officer of the German Armed Forces, the Wehrmacht straight away. You do know how to win a victory for your side."

'The translator translated, and Hitler and his coterie looked expectantly at me. How would this small framed, unrecognised, unrewarded Indian take the German bait? If he took it, the Germans would convert it into a great propaganda victory for themselves. Stealing the best hockey player of the British Empire. That would rub the British badly and show Germany in a nice light to the world.

'Tell the Führer that I feel honoured by his generous offer. I am humbled by his consideration. However humble my rank be in the Indian Army, I am an Indian and India is my home. I can only be happy among my own people and on the soil of India.

'"Ach so," said the Führer and he walked on towards the waiting German players.'

Post-independence, the supreme hockey player, Dhyan Chand, retired as a Major from the Indian Army. He is the reigning deity of Indian hockey.